Dark Essence

'To believe in the unbelievable is to give it credence.'

For our lass

'We ourselves are that condition Alesandro and for now we are still that exception.'

Early morning 19th October 2016. Goldworthy Street. Reading.

Alexander frowned, it was not what he had expected or wished to see, the windows in darkness. The ancient worn out leather bag in his hand was heavy and having carried it for a distance and for a great deal of time his arms ached. He strode towards the large dirty window the paint of it's frames cracked and peeling, the sign above and just below the shops roof faded and discoloured.

Concetta's Antiques and Curios.

With slow hesitating steps Alexander with Diogo as always his shadow made his way closer to the old but imposing building and when near enough lent forward and put his forehead against the window. He placed his hands over the top of his eyes above his eyebrows and held his breath so as not to steam up the surface, he could just make it out in the gloom, the one thing he had hoped not to see. On the top of a crammed with objet d'art shelfon the back wall it stood half in half out of the shadows and in a wide gap that if you didn't know any better would think it had made for itself. The figure, a bronze figure of a bent and withered old lady supporting her frail body with a cane. Nearest it on the left was a clock, a brass alarm clock that wasn't brass at all but he could tell even from this distance that light metal, cheap and sharp edged. On the right of it a pair of vases, tall, flowerless, both decorated with transferred smudges of no doubt gaudy colours that were mercifully subdued by the lack of light in the shop. Some of these objects Alexander could recall others he could not and yet he had been responsible for their being in the shop, all of them at some time or another... each and every item had been, *taken, retrieved, removed,* by Alexander and brought to the shop, each one had deserved its notoriety in one way or another...Alexander drew his head back, took his hands away and checked for the third time in as many minutes. The sign on the door did indeed say 'Closed'. It was a weekday, all the neighbouring shops were open only this one was closed. He would have to come back, he could not chance it, he had his own set of keys but he could not interrupt his mother as she was obviously otherwise occupied. Diogo's apartment was not too far away, cramped but dry and warm the two men made their way there.

Early morning, 20th October 2016 Goldworthy Street. Reading.

Alexander with Diogo at his side, quickened his step. A light was on he could see it as he approached. The bell on the door chimed as he entered, the Open/ Closed sign swayed on its twine swing and tapped the glassed before settling, Closed side now facing out to the street. Alexander eyes went directly to the cluttered shelf on the back wall...the gap between the clock and the vases appeared to be wider but he was sure it was only because the bronze figure of the old lady, he was relieved to see, was no longer between them.

 'You are early back Alesandro, a whole day early, I am barely prepared, I have had to' A pause ensued before she continued...' lately, I have had to delve too deep, travel too far within the restraints of my mind, it sometimes takes more time than I can withstand, I am getting too old'.

 The voice came from behind the stained pitted counter, in the semi darkness stood a wizened elderly lady, humped backed, white haired and grasping in one gnarled hand a gold-tipped wooden cane....Alexander had expected her words, he was already aware of what she was to say, what had been on her mind, he raised the ancient leather bag and placed it on the counter, her eyes took it in and were at once intense but she made no movement towards it.

'I see you have been successful again in your errand?' Only now did she glance at Diogo but no words passed between them just a knowing nod.

'You will stop to eat with your mother, I see little of you these days, maybe our work is becoming too much of our lives'

For now Alexander ignored the plea in his mothers voice, letting his eyes wander to the shelf on the back wall to the obvious gap between the items stored thereupon. His mother followed his gaze with her own and immediately sensed his concern. The bronze figure of the old lady was gone, it was one that Alexander knew had emitted strong 'dark essence' and it had been cause for concern to him...

'It is done Alesandro trust me, the object you are searching for is now void of its previous energies, I am old not weak or lacking in my '*shall we say talents*' now come and breakfast with me I have another errand for you and Diogo to talk of'

Alexander turned his head to search and confirm the shop was, apart from the three of them empty and then turned back to face his mother.

'You must call me Alexander mother, Alexander and nothing else, please remember, next time there may be others abroad and to them I am always Alexander'

Concetta looked dismayed, she lowered her eyes and Alexander could not help but see tears welling up in them...

'I feel it wont have to be for much longer, you know our work has to be protected..'

As he spoke he released the leather drawstring, placed his hand into the top of the bags open neck and carefully lifted from it its fragile contents. Concetta Constantine knew exactly where in the shop she needed to place it for now and without another word took it there.

--- --- --- --- ---

The journey had been as he'd hoped, largely uneventful. From Ostend to the City of Dinant 90 Kilometres south of Brussels the train passed through some beautiful Belgian countryside. Alexander was grateful for this; it meant that the people sharing his carriage had eyes only for it, not for them. He took the crumpled missive his mother had given him from the top pocket of his sharply starched jacket and read it for the hundredth time, scrutinising each sentence for any trace or sense of the writer falsifying, mocking or simply lying, again he found none. Diogo had eyes only for trees on the other side of the trains window that sped across his vision, made transient imprints in his mind and then disappeared for ever.

--- --- --- --- ---

My new Friend Dr. Alesandro Constatine.

With many good wishes to you. I read with you many good thoughts and feel it must be I write to yourself. I read many books from your hand and many items from magazines you write inside. You tell of many tales and stories of the evil of many things. The luck charms, talismans and amulets and the dooms of them. I have of such a thing. You tell you no of the histories of such things and how to battle these things. I have a curse of old thing and my terrors are many. My son, Arne have death because of curse of old thing, they try destroy but no. You write you can destroy and not have death. I beg of you my new friend Dr. Alesandro Costatine, you have do what you write I have have much gratitude to you. I beg you Dr. Alesandro, please bring me your help.

Mevr. Lotte Jassen

Rue du Meandre

Dinant.

Belgium.

Alexander closed his eyes and sank back into his reasonably comfortable seat, satisfied in the knowledge that to the outside world he would look no more than the fatigued traveller making

use of the time to rest. But nothing could be further from the truth. With the missive now pressed firmly between the open palm of his left hand and his breast under the cover of his jacket Alexander having read it again with his eyes could now revisit its *'dark essence'* with his mind. Soon he would be within its aura, a thought that stirred him automatically to feel for the empty leather bag that he had placed on the floor between his feet, it was there, as he knew it would be. For the last few kilometres the train moved aggravatingly slowly, his fellow passengers eyes began to search for his as if they could possibly somehow know the purpose of his travelling and he grew uncomfortably warmer. A voiced question came from one side of the carriage not for him but his diminutive companion who's eyes were still firmly fixed to the trains window.

'Are you travelling far sir?' Diogo made not the slightest movement in reply, Alexander turned towards the speaker and responded on his behalf as he always did.

'Alexander lied, not for the first, not for the last, 'The gentleman to whom you direct your question is profoundly deaf sir'

Diogo was a man of very few words and he was selective as to who he spoke to. Maybe it was the tone of his voice or the look in Alexander's eyes but no more conversation ensued. Dinant could not be too far away but the feeling that he was not welcome to visit it began to be harder and harder to dispel.

Alexander was no stranger to these emotions and sensations having endured them on many occasions before. And still the train slowed and still his body's blood warmed. 'Dinant, Dinant'

the mechanical words roused him from his reverie and instantly became his mother's voice alerting him to the promise of another impending liaison, the tightening and twisting of his nerves becoming one with the screeching of the trains rusting brakes.

--- --- --- --- ---

He had been vaguely aware of the train in the background pulling out of Dinant station but that was quite a while ago. They had taken their time crossing the footbridge over the River Meuse and making their way to the address in the missive but now an urgency had taken the place of trepidation. Alexander and Diogo's hastened footsteps echoed along the cobbles of Rue du Meandre as they approached the building he could now see without looking for, his senses were now his guide. Alexander climbed the four concrete steps to its entrance raised his fist and his hollow knock was thunder in the silence. The door was ajar and the force of his hand against the wooden panel enough to swing it open on its hinges, Alexander stood on the threshold letting his eyes adapt to the shadows. Diogo remained at street level, Alexander would summon him if he were required. Save for the dull yellow glimmer from the few tapers spread frugally there was precious little light in the chilled and damp room. In the centre stood a heavy wooden table bearing the worn scars of a thousand cuts, indents and aged black unidentifiable stains. At each side of the table high back chairs, three of which stood empty their upright spokes and arched backs distorting the flickering candle light to make dancing shadows on the cold stone floor and shadowed walls. On the fourth chair was seated Lotte Jassen, hunched over, with her forehead on the table top, her face hidden under long greying and matted hair and both hands closed tight over her ears. The dancing shadows avoided her, the darker ones claimed her and she was grateful for that small mercy. Alexander took another step into the cramped room and was met with a cornucopia of loud and disturbing sounds coming from somewhere above his head, he looked up and saw dust motes cascading from the cracks in the ceiling. A woman's voice, imploring, beseeching, a man's sobbing, the scrapping of wooden bed legs against the floor all emanating from a stairway leading to the buildings upper floor. Invisible to Alexander the large oak door at the top of the stairs slowly opened with its groaning hinges protesting at every determined push from behind. Elise stepped across its threshold and silhouetted starkly by the rooms own light stood motionless in waves of hideous sobs that pulsed at her back. Below in the semi dark still sitting at the table and paralysed with fear Lotte finally felt the presence now standing at her side, she took her hands from her ears and dared to look up.

Through eyes that were blurred with tears she saw the figure of a man, a man she had never seen before in her life, a man she knew to be Dr. Alesandro Constantine. Lotte opened her mouth to speak to him but the words were just not there and a nauseating dizziness threatened to take her consciousness. And the voice again from somewhere upstairs, took both hers and Alexander's attention and as one their heads turned and their eyes looked into the darkness.

'Arne wants you mother, I can no longer control him, you must come to him, I am afraid mother, I am so afraid, please…

'I must go to her, I must go to them both'

As she spoke Lotte struggled to stand, pushing the chair back with her rigid thighs as she did so. Pain shot up her left arm and gathered in a cold paralysing mass in her shoulders and neck. She tried to move her legs, tried to lever herself up from the chair and then felt hands on her shoulder and under her arms. Alexander attempted to raise the old woman from the table but a solid terror held her in its paralysing grip. And then the female voice seemingly from a thousand miles away came to her again.

'Mother, mother please, I need you here, it is happening again, please, please'

From somewhere behind those frantic words, other sounds, guttural choking, racked with vicious bouts of uncontrolled coughing and retching. Lotte finally managed to stand, she pushed back the hair that had fallen across her eyes and was sticking to the wet tears flowing down her cheeks. She took wavering steps towards the sound of Elise's pleading cries..

'Mother, please, you must come up here I need you up here, Arne needs you up here....'

Restraining the elderly lady as gently as he could Alesandro looked over her shoulder caught a glimpse of Diogo still standing on the steps to the entrance of the building and with a single nod of his head bade him enter. As the two men guided Lotte back to her chair and coaxed her into it Alexander placed both his hands on her shoulders and looked into her eyes..

'Tell her help is at hand'

And with that he made his way to the foot of the stairs listening to Lotte's words at his back.

'Help is at hand, Elise, help is at hand allow him to enter'.

With Diogo sitting at Lotte's side at the table, Alexander took the stairs two by two toward the landing, grasping tightly onto the balustrade to gain as much upward motion as possible, the leather bag's handles wrapped tightly around his wrist. Elise was standing in front and above him, dressed in long flowing robes that were shapeless and grey, in her hand she held a flickering candle the sallow skin of her face illuminated by its feeble light. Alexander gestured her to one side of the open door and put his index finger to his lips. Elise fell silent and did as he bade allowing him clear access to the room, he stepped past and without hesitation she handed him the candle. As the feeble light partially illuminated the room the man on the bed raised his shoulders and turned his head towards it and even in the semi darkness Alexander could see his mouth forming the words...

'Help me, whoever you are please help me, it will not release me, the standing stone has hold of my mind, it is taking my mind'.

Alexander took a couple of tentative steps towards the figure on the bed when another voice, not carried to his ears on the air but deep in his own mind assailed him.

'To quoque nuper' Too Late.

Now Alexander could sense the source, and although the shadows conspired to hide it a large stone bust with unseeing eyes standing tall on the top of a tall book filled bookcase somehow made itself conspicuous.

'To quoque nuper' Too late

Again words somewhere deep in his mind, his voice was steady and he replied as he took a step forwards, ' You are mistaken, I am not late at all'

'*Derelinquamus'* Leave

'It is not I that will be leaving it is you' Alexander felt a shift in the air, an icy cooling of his skin.

'*Derelinquamus'* Leave

'No' replied Alexander, ' I will go nowhere,I have my work to do'

'*Hoc est ut mori* This man is to die.

Alexander took a step toward the bookcase and as he fixed his eyes on the bust, he raised the leather bag and opened its neck.

Hoc est ut mori

Alexander answered the voice in his head once again.

'This man is not dying , I defy you, you will not have your murderous way this time'.

Raising a hand he took the bust under its protruding chin, carefully placed it into the bag and pulled the drawstring tight. When the voice came echoing in his brain a final time Alexander knew at once its unveiled threat.

'*Enmus iterum conveniant'*

'Our kind will meet with you again'.

He was on the landing, the only sound a resonating sobbing coming from the room downstairs.

'It is over, go to him, he needs comforting, Arne needs you now'

Alexander made to hand her the candle and gestured with his eyes that she should take it and it was now permissible for her to enter her brother's room. Elise made no move, she just stood looking at Alexander's face and then into the dark space now at his back.

'I promise you this evil cannot claim him now'. As he spoke

Alexander raised the leather bag, held it up aloft whilst Elise breathed in its contents dying scent and then he lowered it down to rest again at his side. Wordlessly Elise took the proffered candle in her shaking hand, looked again into the inner eyes of a man she now could quite easily give all her trust and stepped without hesitation into her brother's room.

'Arne, Arne, it is I, Elise, fear no more, the evil is gone, it is no more, its hold on you is now broken'.

'It is done?'

Diogo's question rose up to meet him as Alexander was making his way down the staircase into the fractured candle light of the cottages lower room. Diogo was now standing over the seated form of the old lady, his hands gently resting on her shoulders. Lotte Jassen slowly getting to her feet turned her face towards the stairs and the descending Alexander, tears streaming from her eyes. Crossing herself feverishly she made her stumbling way towards him, a torrent of words issuing from her lips in a language neither Alexander nor Diogo understood and did not need to. Alexander raised the leather bag and it's contents once again for Diogo's perusal and received a nod of acceptance from the small Portuguese man..'It is done' he said 'Concetta will have more work to keep her busy this days end.

Part Two

Sitting on the too small hard wooden seat with the set of glaring white lights shining directly into his eyes Alexander wondered how this night of his *'Night of Insight'* would go. Concetta had made the 'booking' many days ago, after someone called Alison had contacted her by letter...*it is written by one who has suffered the evil manifestations of a 'dark essence' of that I have no doubt, you must feel it for yourself directly to know the way to respond my son, you must attend at all cost'*....His mothers words echoed in his mind and as a result Alexander found himself in the small Berkshire Village of Buckleberry. Whoever that person was, was in dire need of their help, his mother knew this and his mother was never mistaken. The rows of similar small hard wooden seats facing him were slowly being filled and the stuffy auditorium became busy with the sounds of stifled coughing and low mutterings. No-one paid any attention to the single, shuffling figure of Diogo as he made his way to a chair at the end of the back row, his demeanour one of invisibility.

Alexander tried not to catch his eye or any other of his *'would be'* audience; experience had taught him that it would be a mistake for his senses to tune into any one person too hastily. Another darting look at the oversized electric clock on the back wall told him that it was just after two minutes to eight, time to place his leather bag on the floor by the stage where he would remember to pick it up later. The man with the long hair and

longer beard adjusted the mike fixed to the rostrum centre stage for the fifth time in as many minutes and Alexander caught the sound and movement to his left with a quick deft flick of his head.

'Good evening all and welcome once again to another edition of 'Night of Insight' here at Bucklebury Village Hall, with me Barry Sedgewick and the Bucklebury Village Institute. The applause from the half empty hall echoed against the wood and plaster walls of the building and Alexander stiffened noticeably in his uncomfortable seat. Barry Sedgewick allowed the applause to die down for longer than necessary enjoying the moment, when he raised the mike once again to his mouth it was with a theatrical flourish.

'It is great to see so many people here tonight and I am sure for those who have made the effort to come out you will not be disappointed'

Alexander squirmed in his seat at the word 'effort' but kept his eyes down and out of the nuisance glare; he let the drone of Barry Sedgewick's introduction go over his head and almost missed his cue.

'And so, with no further ado, I welcome our distinguished guest speaker for this evening on the often ridiculed subject of 'dark essence' Dr. Alesandro Constantine'.

Alexander stood to a generous if not over exuberant applause catching the scornful glint of derision in his introducer's eyes and repeating in his mind the words 'often ridiculed' which

neither man had used in their initial meeting. After a while the applause died down and with it its hollow echo, Alexander acknowledged his appreciation with a fleeting smile a nodding gesture and then for a good twenty seconds let the silence have its effect. The lights dimmed, a chair leg scraped along the wooden floorboards, someone coughed and from the second row back sitting straight backed on her too small hard wooden seat Alison Cleaver's eyes locked onto the man's on the stage, and momentarily his on hers. He was to go through his usual repertoire asking the audience questions at the appropriate moments, fawning sometimes at their responses just to keep up interest. Some of the answers he knew he would receive would be surprising, some interesting, none apart from maybe one or two worthwhile of his pursuance; in the meantime he found it harder and harder to ignore Alison Cleaver's stare, her invisible pleading but he was required to do so. For appearances sake he was paid to. Walking to the centre of the stage he held his arms out wide and then brought them down making a triangle of his hands under his chin, he paused and took a huge breath, when he spoke it felt to him as if someone else was speaking.

'Good evening one all, and to begin may I thank you for your much appreciated warm welcome. We are here tonight to embark on a journey of discovery, a journey that will no doubt evoke many different opinions, views, and indeed questions. All I ask of you is to come to me with your minds open and a willingness in your hearts to listen to my words before judging, dismissing or indeed ridiculing me. My talk to you tonight, as you know, is concerning my theory of what I believe to be the phenomenon I call 'dark essence, or dark energy'. It is my profound hope that you are here tonight having read maybe one or two of my many publications on this subject or for your own reasons, an interest in gaining more information about it. So, if we are all sitting reasonably comfortably', Alexander paused to allow a ripple of subdued laughter to rise from his audience'.. 'To start the proceedings permit me to ask you all a simple question that may sound extraneous but I assure you is pertinent.' Alexander took a couple of steps towards the edge of the stage, widened the forced smile already adorning his face and spoke loudly and clearly.

'Tell me has anyone here ever had a meaningful if one-sided relationship with a doll, a teddy bear, a plastic duck? Has anyone here ever had an invisible friend?' Please do not be shy in coming forward because I assure you I would guess at least 80% if not more of you have.' He gave the audience time to answer, to consider, to summon up the confidence to react, he searched their faces for the responses he hopefully expected, at last a hand went up in the first row and Alexander immediately zeroed in on its owner.

'May I be so bold as to ask you your name?'

'Maureen' said the woman looking apprehensively at the people sitting in the row either side of her 'Mrs Maureen Austin', Alexander's smile was now just for Maureen, he placed his arms at his chest, the tips of the fingers of both hands meeting to form a triangle under his chin, 'Thank you Maureen, may I call you Maureen?'

The middle aged woman was silent at first giving the distinct impression she wished she hadn't put herself in the spot she now found herself in. She murmured in the affirmative. Alexander was quick to encourage her input, he held her with his eyes and gestured her to her feet. She stood slowly, wary of looking nowhere but at him, her voice when it came was barely audible.

'I had a cat, not a real one of course but a cuddly toy, he slept in my bed and ..'

Alexander smiled warmly to bolster the lady's confidence, he took a measured step towards her speaking to only her as he did so.

'Maureen, did you talk to your cat, did you have a name for your cat, was he your friend?'

'Alfie' the lady responded, 'his name was Alfie and of course I spoke to him he..' She fell silent, she'd spoken enough, she felt herself redden, the audience would laugh at her, she made to sit down but Alexander held her attention with his warm friendly smile.

'Alfie was your friend wasn't he, of course you spoke to him and he spoke to you did he not ?'

The lady called Maureen answered despite herself...

'Yes, we talked a lot'

Alexander shifted his eyes to those of another woman sitting only a few chairs away, he had read her signs.

'And you madam, I can see that you also had a friend you conversed with did you not?...and may we have your name?'

She was older, much older, she did not stand but her voice carried well.

'My name is Margaret and I don't mind telling you, if it weren't for Nellie I would not be here now.'

Alexander remained silent but in some way prompting, he sensed the older woman, Margaret, had much more to say and he was eager for her to do so.

'Nellie was always with me, even when I thought all the others were gone, Nellie stayed with me. I could feel the earth shake and was so frightened the flickering lights would go off altogether, but Nellie told me that even if they did she'd still be with me.'

The audience was his, his and hers and much to Alexander's gratification the older woman stood to take to centre stage.

'It was during the war you see, we were in the shelters, the ones with the railway tracks that dad always told us kids to stay away from. Me, my brother Ronald and Ma. The Germans were bombing us see and we had to keep down there safe. Sometimes I'd wake up, it was the noise you see. People were all scrunched up and sometimes Ma and Dad gone or nowhere to been seen. Ronald would be mixed up with the other boys playing marbles or climbing the holes in the walls....Nellie was always there, telling me the Germans couldn't reach us with their bombs and all...Nellie was always there, she..'

It was going well, the big clock at the back of the hall told him his hours 'talk' was over half way through, soon Alexander would be asking the questions that he had spent up till now encouraging his audience to answer '*the other side of the coin*' as he often put it. Soon things would be getting interesting. From her seat two rows back Alison Cleaver was well aware that the mood in the hall was soon to change dramatically. Alexander had walked across the stage and was facing the elderly female speaker, it was time to interrupt her monologue and he was subtle and efficient at doing it...he spoke as she was in mid sentence.

'You were very lucky indeed madam to have had such a marvellous friend during what must have been such terrible times'

His voice was loud, incisive and he held his arms out as if trying to embrace the elderly woman who although nobody in the audience including herself had been aware, was cut off abruptly in midstream. Alexander was speaking again giving no time for answer. 'Nellie must have afforded you great comfort, she was obviously a good friend but have you ever stopped to consider what it would have been like if she had been an enemy?'

A bemused silence fell over the hall, Alexander used it to add volume to his voice.

'Ridiculous as it may sound, what if your friend 'Nellie' had been malicious, a demon, an evil spirit, malevolent and wicked?'

'Nellie wasn't like that all', responded the older lady,

'Nellie loved me and I loved her, what are you talking about?'

Embarrassed by her own sudden outburst Margaret was quick to find her seat and make herself once more just part of the audience. Alexander moved his eyes across the faces that stared opened mouthed at him, his words echoed against the hall's wood panelling and high beamed roof, he had the audience where he wanted them.

'Ladies and Gentlemen I now come to the essence of my talk to you tonight and I make no apologise for that deliberate pun.'

'Due to lack of time I have only been able to exhibit two examples of what I term 'dark essence' and I thank the charming Maureen and Margaret for helping me with this. Both ladies have illustrated what I am convinced is nothing strange to any of you here tonight, I am sure nothing untoward. We all go through life with this feeling of a certain kindred spirit, a relationship if you will, with inanimate objects. You may have a statue in your garden that watches you every time pass it, a vase that has been 'in the family' for as long as you can remember sitting on your mantelpiece, you may be aware of a certain tree in a field that you have the overwhelming urge to

touch or talk to whenever you walk by, it may even talk to you, or even more bizarrely an object that demanded your attention, insisted your obedience, was capable of instilling in you a sense of irrational fear of it.' Alexander paused, looking around his audience letting his words sink in before continuing...

'Is it so far from the realms of comprehension that if an item can be of a friendly disposition it could also be of an unfriendly one, if an object can somehow radiate an aura of warmth and well-being it could also be capable of the converse ?'

A silence fell across the hall and after what seemed an age an arm was raised and a voice heard from the midst of the audience.

'Would the Dr. suggest that all inanimate objects possess some degree of....'

'The owner of the female voice asking the question paused, her hand still up, her mouth open, when she managed to find the words, she lowered her arm and continued with her inquiry... 'some degree of what you call 'dark essence?'

Alexander cleared his throat, it was a question that he had responded to a thousand times before and he would have to be careful not to sound too trite.

'I believe that it is incredibly rare for any object to radiate any form of 'dark essence' to an unreceptive person or persons, having said that a person given the gift wanted or unwanted of such receptiveness could easily succumb to the *dark essence*

emitted'

From the midst of the audience a man stood up, bearded and well dressed, he had a discernible German accent and his question took Alexander completely by surprise, it was a condition he had experienced rarely, never written about or wanted to discuss with anyone else, it was a subject he'd rather not dwell upon.

'Would Dr. Constantine refute or confirm the existence of S.D.E.. 'Spontaneous Dark Essence', whereby essence energies can be merged together by exposure to the purest of evil and in doing so making them far more powerful, far more potent'.

The man sat down pleased with the reaction his words had obviously caused, he made a note in his little note book and placed it back in the pocket of his jacket. Murmurings and the odd cough filled the room as this question was absorbed, Alexander would pause only slightly to allow this to happen, experience had taught him that if he was to be stretched at all it would be at this juncture. In answer he continued.

'In my vast experience of dealing with persons affected by this extreme or violent phenomena, I can assure you that what we talk about being a mere energy can it's said apparently manifest itself into something far more tangible, far more physical as in S.D.E. I have in my possession accounts of *Spontaneous dark energy*' being responsible for actual and in real time violent activity...although I hasten to add it is extremely rare. It is at this point in my talk that I would like to introduce to you a

person who may have had experience as such and who has made it his life's pledge to save others from the dreadful plight he himself endured.

It was a while before a volunteer stagehand directing one of the stage lights found him but when the small man at the end of the back row stood the audience as one turned their heads and eyes in his direction. In the new shadows Alexander sat down and became part of them. Diogo could not help but blink as the fierce white light impinged against his retinas and he was immensely relieved he could see nothing at all of the audience. Diogo was by nature a shy man and to talk to so many would once have been impossible for him to do. His voice carried well for one of his stature and his old accent barely discernible, it had been a long time ago since the Portuguese sun had warmed the brown skin of his back...Diogo took a deep breath, lifted his chin and without any form of unnecessary introduction, began to speak, attaining his audiences full attention immediately.

'We were but children, playing hunters and stalkers under the hot homeland sun on the banks of the river Limia. For my sister Leonor, brother Anacleto and I the youngest Diogo, the days were long and exciting. We'd take cold bifana and fruit wrapped in cloth and search for montros in the murky waters and reed covered banks. The Limia was ours, cool for the days sun and full of fish for our varas de pescar'

Diogo paused his eye's searched the audience and the glimmer of a smile at a distant memory touched his lips as he translated...'Fishing poles'

And then the smile vanished and his words were once more filling the listening silence of the hall.

'Anacelto found it, he lifted it from the waters murk and held it high letting the dirtied waters flow from a hole in its side down his naked arms and over the thin ribs of his chest.

'I have found the tesouro, the gold tesouro, we will all be much rica, we will buy big food, we will buy joias for mamae and tabaco for papai'

He shouted and laughed at the same time, 'We will all be *rica*'.

Leonor grabbed at my arm and raising mud from the rivers bank we ran towards the jumping splashing idiota that was my brother and made as if to praise him as if he were a god. It would be a while before the childish excitement and manic laughter turned to utter exhaustion and over took us and we as one sunk to our knees in the cooling waters.

'We should make our way home' it was Leonor and her body was covered in the small bumps of growing cold. On the soft sand we gathered up our bifana cloth and sandals it was just as we were leaving Anacelto remembered his find, his tesouro. '

' 'Wait' he cried at our backs as Leonor and I started off for home. We ran from him, the sound of our childish laughter bouncing off the Limia's waters and echoing along the banks. If only Anacelto had followed us and left that reliquia do mal in its deserved place in the mud of the river's bed.' The silence in the hall was thick and expectant, when Alexander's voice came from the shadows most of the audience actually jumped in their chairs.

'We now surmise the object Anacelto retrieved from the waters of the river was merely the remains of a jug or vase..nothing more nothing less, but in the children's imagination something magical.'

Having spoken, Alexander was once again, as silent as the shadows. Diogo, took a single step away from the row of chairs at his side looked into the darkness where he knew Alexander to be, then fixed his eyes once again onto the audience cleared his throat and spoke.

'It was nothing, as Alexander says but it was heavy, the shape of a vase with holes bored into its sides and one handle missing, it was nothing'

As he spoke he made gestures with his hands forming a vase like shape in the air and putting one hand above the other to give an idea of the height of the object. 'It was soon that my brother Anacelto had cleaned and polished it's surface, a pattern in faded colours tried to make itself seen through a thousand years of time but still remained mostly invisible' He held it up to his face and peered through one of the holes in its side grinning like a maniaco. Our father teased Anacelto, 'My boy, you have saved us all from starvation, it is our salvation, this *'tesouro de ouro macico' We will take it to the market in the city and sell it for um milhao de escudo'*

'We all laughed, including Anacelto, if my mother laughed with us I cannot remember but I do remember her telling my brother to take his tesouro back to the Limia, where it belonged, no, she did not tell him, it sounded as if she begged him.'

'It was strange to hear my mother's voice sound the way it had, I paused to look at her, to catch her eyes but they were fixed on the piece of broken ceramics. Our father picked the tesouro from Anacelto's hands and held it over his head, he did a little dance as his voice rang out.'

'Anacelto's tesoura e um presente de Deus , olha como brilha ouro'

'Leonor was now dancing too, proudly echoing my fathers words but in strange childish tongue. 'Anacelto's treasure is a gift from God, look how it shines like gold'

'When my mother screamed all the dancing and laughter ceased immediately, a coldness filled the room and her body hit the floor with a sound I will never forget as long as I live.....' Diogo was all of a sudden silent, the hall was silent and then Alexander's voice came out of the shadows once again.

'Be seated my friend Diogo I will see to it to spare you any further torturous recollections.'

Diogo took a step sideways found his chair with his arms at his back and lowered himself wordlessly into it. As he did so the spotlight left him in the shadows and at once found a standing Alexander.

'Diogo's mother died that very day, his father less than a week later, after another few months when Leonor's constant wailing became her only words she was secured in uma casa para os insanos...where she will remain for the rest of her life. To this day Anacelto has never been seen.'

Stifled gasps and nervous coughs from the spellbound audience filled the hall and Alexander fell silent inviting what he was expecting, questions, and he was not to be disappointed.

'Dr. Alexander, are you seriously suggesting that all that happened to this, this unfortunate man and his family' ..the audience member with his hand raised paused to look in the direction of the now shadowed Diogo before continuing 'was somehow connected to the...'*treasure*' his brother Anacelto found in the bed of a river?'

Alexander's answer was immediate and succinct.

'I know it was.'

A few yards of floor space and a couple of rows of chairs away Alison Cleaver listened to every word spoken by Dr. Alexander and her eyes never left his. He was speaking again and she sensed to her, directly to her, the vast majority of the audience had somehow drifted away into the peripheral gloom of the hall. It was as his mother had told him, *'She will find you Alesandro, she will find you and you will know her'* And now he was speaking again.

'The 'dark essence ' that is created by some object's, antiques, objet d'art, artefacts, can be of immense power, unseen and yet destructive, an unholy force that in some cases proves to be unstoppable. Although Anacelto's find was only a broken segment of such an object its power was still very much so intact.' A gasp from the shadows followed by a nervous cough, the scrape of a wooden legged chair against the polished wooden floor and from the stage Alexander voice a mere whisper.

'Many of you will snigger at my words of tonight, maybe you snigger now, that is how it must be but I would like to leave you all tonight with at least the idea that there maybe a modicum of truth in what I have spoken of. '

And then to a smattering of nervous applause the hall's lights came up, people began to stand escaping the constricting wooden chairs with aching leg muscles and relieved sighs. In the dying echo of his own voice Dr. Alexander let his eyes rest entirely on Alison Carver's sitting two rows of chairs away from him, he could sense the tension in her muscles the fear barely contained in her taunt body. He watched her turn her head as a stranger's voice from somewhere near her in the audience shook her from her thoughts.

'Excuse me please miss'

He watched her being reluctantly ushered along towards the hall's exit doors and the cold air that now blew through them.

Alison Cleaver shuffled out of the hall, her fingers clenching and

unclenching her heart racing, her mind in turmoil, praying that soon Dr. Alexander Constantine would come to her and her alone. Behind her Diogo had joined Alexander and both men were making their way off the stage to Barry Sedgewick who was in deep conversation with the man with the long hair and longer beard.

'What have we got next week Baz? I hope its better than...'

Alexander was certain that the question asked of 'Baz' by the bearded man was intended for him and Diogo to hear, he ignored them, picked up the small leather bag he had left at the foot of the stage and with Diogo at his side made for the halls doors.

--- --- --- --- ---

'It had to be my way Miss Cleaver, I do not expect you to understand my proviso or indeed my motives but I assure you all was as it had to be'

Alison looked into Alexander's eyes and saw something in them that somehow quelled her anxiety, her trepidation, she had written to this man's mother with a desperate plea for help and here he was, she could ask for no more. They were standing in the silver white light of the small gravelled car park of the village hall the sound of car doors being closed all around them. Some of his once audience stopped briefly to nod appreciation, or convey gestures of mere politeness, most passed by with just a glance of curiosity. The man who had been the guest speaker

was now in deep conversation with a young lady and it was so intense that those few that wanted further intercourse with Dr. Alexander Constantine were obliged to keep their silence, make their ways across the crunching gravel and disappear into their appropriate cars.

Part Three

Alexander guided the large Volvo estate between the gateless posts and brought the car to a halt on the rutted gravelled drive of the small cottage. Behind him on the back seat Diogo was fast asleep, the retelling of his traumatic story always resulted in his total exhaustion. Beside him in the passenger seat Alexander could sense the young lady's body stiffen and her breath caught in her throat as she opened her mouth to speak.

'I cannot go in there again, I just cannot go back in there, I can't explain why my mother may be in some kind of danger, but I'm afraid Alexander, terrified'.

Alexander reached for the cars ignition and turned the key, the engine died and the immediate silence was deafening. In the bright white glow of the cars interior light Alison watched as Alexander turned in his seat to face her and felt his hands find hers.

'You have to be brave Alison, do exactly as I've told you and no harm will befall you as I promised.'

Alison recalled the words Alexander had spoken to her less than 20 minutes ago in the car park of the Buckleberry Village Hall. They had left her car there and driven to her mother's house in Alexander's, she would pick her own up in the morning, in the daylight. For now she found herself sitting in a strange car with two men she'd only recently met staring up through the darkness surrounding her mother's home a sickening fear radiating through her stomach. From an upstairs window a dull yellow glow was visible through a gap in the curtains the lower part of the building was in total darkness. Alexander gently took his hands from Alison's and reached between the two front seats to retrieve the leather bag he knew to be there, Diogo made not the slightest movement. Alexander unclipped his seatbelt, Alison jumped in her seat at the sound of it, hers was still fastened and it would take all of her will to release it. Alexander leant on the Volvo's driver side door and it opened allowing a draft of cold air into the car. Alison's fingers finally felt the cold steel of her seat belt. And then the hissed voice came from a black hole that had opened up in the shadowed wall of the cottage and the figure now appearing in it..

'They are watching, they can see you, they can see you all, you cannot stop them, go away.'

'Mother, its me, Alison, I have Alexander here, he has come to help us, he knows what to do mother'

Alison spoke as she stepped from the car, her mother's frightened voice giving her the impetus to ignore the fear that had up until then frozen her muscles and chilled her blood. No longer a hiss, but a plea, carried on a wave of terror .. her mother's voice came to her once again.

'Ali, go away, save yourself, you do not belong here, you should not be here, do not...'

Alison heard the crunching of gravel underfoot and was aware that Alexander had left his side of the car and was standing at her shoulder, his confident voice filled the cold night air with an unnaturally calm aura.

'Mrs Cleaver, My name is Dr. Alexander Constatine, I am with your daughter, I am here in response to your letter, do you remember your letter, requesting my assistance, well - here I am, I know I can assist you with this horror that has befallen you all.'

Alison felt Alexander's hand on her lower arm, he was guiding her forward, away from the car and the sleeping Diogo towards the black silhouette in the shadows that was her mother. 'Mrs Cleaver you have nothing to fear I....'

It was then that the upstairs window of the cottage shattered sending a fountain of splintered glass in every direction and plunging the whole building into total darkness. Alison's scream escaped her mouth before she could prevent it and in an instant she had pulled herself free from Alexander's hold and was

taking urgent steps towards the prone figure on the ground at the cottages door. Alexander could do no more than stare at the gaping hole in the wall that was once a window, an icy chill of alien fear spread itself down his spine, his mind raced...

This 'dark essence' had manifest itself with an actual physical strength, he had previous knowledge of it and with that came certain unaccountable sensations he had never experienced before, he would need to fight to overcome them...and all of a sudden he realised he would need Diogo's help to do it.

In the car Diogo's eyes sprung open, his right temple came into painful contact with the cars side window and for a good few seconds he had no idea where he was. From somewhere in the darkness a woman's scream assailed his ears and in an instant he became aware of his surrounding's. He was inside Alexander's car and he was alone. Diogo leant between the car's front seats and pulled down the dash board glove compartments cover, a couple of seconds rummaging about and his hand felt the cold plastic of the torch he knew to be there. His thumb found the on/off dimple and immediately the cars interior was bathed in over-bright L.C.D. light. A couple of seconds later Diogo was outside the car and in the torches splayed illumination he saw Alexander anxiously turn his head to face him, behind Alexander caught in an umbra of light he glimpsed what looked like a figure prostrate on the gravel.

And then Alexander was speaking, his voice held a strange tremor Diogo had never heard before.

'Diogo, quick, come over here, bring me that torch'

Training the light on the fallen figure Diogo made his way to Alexander's side, the two men exchanged meaningful glances and followed in Alison's wake as fast as they could. The crunch of their heavy footfalls on the gravel drowning out the sounds emanating from the black yaws that were the cottages windows. Alison was kneeling at her mother's shoulders her arms cradling the old woman's head and upper body, Alexander was relieved to hear the two women quietly talking. Diogo had taken a few steps closer to the cottage and was staring at one of the upstairs windows, he turned his head and his face lit up in the light of Alexander's torch.

'It is up there' he mouthed gesturing with an upward flick of his eyes.

Before either men could move Alison Cleaver was imploring that they helped her with her mother...

--- --- --- --- ---

Diogo held the car's back door open as Alexander and Alison helped the old lady onto the back seat, the bright interior light revealing her pallid skin and contorted features. She was murmuring incoherently and clutching her daughter's arm with the bloodless fingers of both her hands.

'You stay in the car with your mother young lady, we will not be long'.

Alison Cleaver did not need to be told twice and gave Alexander a weak smile as she pulled the cars door closed and took her mother into both arms. Diogo had made his way to the boot, opened it and took out the old leather bag never taking his eyes from the dark formless shape that was the cottage.

--- --- --- --- ---

The paint was flaking but it had obviously been bright red when the sign was first put up, tears of brown rust stained the wood from the screws that were holding it in place. Alexander's torch light illuminated the two words 'Ivy Cottage' as both men made their way through the open door and over the threshold into the narrow hallway of the old building. From inside the car out on the drive way Alison watched intently as the light from the wavering torch beam was swallowed up, disappeared momentarily and then reappeared as dancing shadows emanating from the cottages windows. Between her arms her mother's body stiffened and for a moment she stared around the car as if she had no idea where she was, and when she finally spoke her voice was barely audible...

'I cannot go back in there Ali, those people, those people, looking at me, calling for me to join them...I cannot go back in my home...'and then the sobs were racking her body.

Alison tightened her embrace and gently stroked her mother's head.

--- --- --- --- ---

It was the sound of talking, men talking, low but at the same time loud and it was coming from somewhere through a door on their left along with a fluctuating light that went from bright to nothing. Alexander raised the torch careful to keep it's beam from Diogo's eyes. The two men glanced at each other fleetingly then at the opened door. Alexander stepped away into the shadows and made his way through the door, deeper into the room and switched the television off. With the light from the torch chasing away the complete darkness Alexander and Diogo proceeded slowly up the creaking stairs and nearer to what they were both confident was the dark essence's source...They were at the top of the stairs on the heavily carpeted landing when Alexander motioned to Diogo to hand him the leather bag, he could see even in the sporadic light from the torch the ancient hieroglyphics on the bags heavily creased surface coming to life once again. It, as he, was preparing. Almost at the end of the landing they were confronted by two doors directly opposite each other, without hesitation both men ignored one of them. Icy cold air from the glassless window rushed towards him as Alexander entered the old lady's bedroom with Diogo close behind him, both men involuntarily flinched as the door behind them suddenly slammed shut and the torch in Alexander's hand went out. Standing in the now meagre light from the night's moon entering through the broken shards of the window Alexander's own words of earlier that evening came back to him.

'The 'dark essence' that is created by some object's, antiques,

objet d'art, artefacts, can be of immense power, unseen and yet destructive, an unholy force that in some cases proves to be unstoppable. 'Unstoppable', Surely not for him, for his mother, in the semi darkness he clutched the leather bags handle tightly and made his way across the floor to what was unmistakably the source of the *'dark essence'*.

--- --- --- --- ---

The skies azure with large cumulus clouds frozen in place, no longer drifting, no longer blown. In the distant background a green bush covered hill rising from fields dotted with the blurred forms of long forgotten cows, heads down silently feeding and ignoring all else as they had been doing for decades. Between a bunched group of gnarled and twisted trees a brook's faint blue and silver waters held still in its babbling, with the capture of time by the artists brush. And in the foreground four people clad in clothes and hats of another era, two men standing, two women sitting in the long grass but all with their backs to the viewer and their eyes fixed on something beyond the paintings reaches. It hung askew on the wall held by a single nail that had been bent by the hangers ineptitude. Probably by an old woman, an old woman who lived in Ivy Cottage and was at this moment sitting with her daughter in his car.

--- --- --- --- ---

'I have no reason to leave this cottage and I have no intentions of doing so'

Alison remembered her mother's words as if it had been only yesterday.

'Jack has been dead for over 10 years now and I am quite capable of looking after myself, get yourself back home to Stephen and the kids and let's not hear any more of this talk'

So when did she start falling apart, when did she start phoning all hours of the day and night?

'No, don't be silly darling, you don't have to come over, I just wanted to talk, don't worry about me, really I'm fine'

'But you sound so nervous, so unhappy mother, what is the matter?

'Its a wonderful painting, Ali, reminds me of when I was a little girl'

'What are you talking about mother, what painting?'

'I've hung it up in my bedroom so I can look at it all the time, nearly bashed my thumb with the hammer though' and then her mother's little giggle. 'Jack would have called me a clumsy clot and put it up for me if Jack was..."

'When did she start talking about the four people in the painting, looking at her laughing at her?'

'Mother it's only a painting, take it down if its upsetting you'

'No Ali I can't you don't understand, I can't, they wont let me'

'Who won't let you mother, who won't let you?'

And then Stephen...'Ali, you can't keep driving over there every other weekend, it's over an hour each way and you are looking so stressed, get her to move in with us and sell that god forsaken old cottage, isn't that what Dr. Davies said, she is not going to get any better living there on her own?'

She had to tell Stephen about her mum's painting, the painting she had bought in a charity shop because she *'felt it talked to her and she liked it'* She talks of nothing else now when she rings me Stephen, this bloody painting, I wish she'd never bought it, she's obsessed with it'

'Painting, painting of what?'

'Oh, something about people looking at her, I don't know....'

'Have a word with Doctor Davies, Ali, I'm sure he will give you some answers, maybe it is time she came to live with us'

'Ali, they are laughing at me, can't you see them, they are turning their heads to jeer and mock me'

'Take the painting down mother please, I'm coming over next week end...'

'I can't, I wont'..And that's when she hung up.

'Have a word with Dr. Davies' Stephen's words echoed in her head,' I'm sure he'll give you some answers'

Alison made the appointment for the following day, Dr Davies only suggested what she had expected him to...maybe her mother needed specialist treatment, would she like him to arrange it for her?

The magazine was on top of the pile on the table in the waiting room, Davies surgery and was opened to the article about Dr. Alesandro Constantine and his work with what he called 'dark essence', Alison took it home with her, Dr. Davies wasn't much help maybe this *Dr. Alesandro Constantine* would be.

--- --- --- --- ---

...In the car on the gravel drive of Ivy Cottage Alison's mother stirred again raised her head and looked at her home just as the flickering light from it's windows went out.

'Damn'

In the sudden darkness Alexander twisted the torch towards his own face and stared into the lens as if by doing so it would miraculously come on again.

Beside him he felt Diogo shift his body closer so the two men were shoulder to shoulder, Diogo put out his hand and took the torch from Alexander's.

'We do not need this now' his voice was calm, unaffected, 'This 'dark essence' has found us'.

--- --- --- --- ---

The sun was high in the sky and it's light shone from the paintings canvas casting an eerie glow across the bedroom's ceiling. As Alexander stood transfixed before it he watched as one by one the people in the foreground turned to stare at him their faces contorted by malevolent smiling.

'This should not be happening'

Alexander gripped the leather bag in a tight fist, looking up into the faces of people that should not be where they were and for the first time in his life feeling real fear.

'What is happening?' And then a movement at his shoulder, Diogo rushing towards the wall, the painting, his arms outstretched, his fingers grabbing frantically at either side of it's frame. He turned his head surprised that his friend had not moved with him.

'The bag Alexander, the bag!'

As in a trance Alexander stood rooted to the spot, the eyes of the people in the picture still boring into his own.

The eyes the eyes, they are staring at me, as one they are looking into my very soul.

'The bag Alexander, open the bag and bring to me quickly'

A brief grunt of effort from the smaller man, the snapping of twine and a scrapping of wood against plaster and then Diogo's raised voice.

'Alexander, I need that bag, now!'

Movement in the semi dark, a shifting of warm air by a blast of icy cold. And then Alexander found himself staring at a blank wall holding a leather bag at arms length that was no longer empty and Diogo standing at his side studying him with a look of total astonishment on his face.

'What happened?' Alexander was asking the dark room...'What just happened?' And then a familiar voice at his side, 'I took the painting down Alexander, I placed it in the bag and gave it to you'

More movement, Diogo pulling open the closed door and both men going through it, the cold air now chasing at their backs, the thud, thud of hurried footfalls on the stairs. They were now in the hall looking out through 'Ivy Cottages' front door at the Volvo parked silently, awaiting them on the gravelled drive. Alexander clutching the leather bag his fingers entwined so tightly in its drawstring that he was unknowingly cutting off their blood supply. Diogo in his shadow already reliving in his mind what he had just witnessed in the old lady's bedroom and trying desperately to ignore. Something he had never seen before, fear on the face of Alexander.

Part Four

'It is very late mother and I am in no mood to argue with you, if you won't go to the hospital, I will take you back home with me tonight and we will talk about all that has happened tomorrow morning.' Alison's mother responded with a subdued nod of her head, it was all she could muster. They were in Alexander's Volvo on the way back to the Village hall to pick up Alison' car. In the boot, the bag containing the painting lay under the nylon netting that Alexander had had fitted to hold securely the various articles that his work demanded more times than not he remove. He had not spoken a word since he and Diogo had made a makeshift job of boarding up the broken windows and made secure the cottage. Alison's car stood alone in the car park illuminated by the Volvo's powerful headlights, Alexander pulled up in front of it and got out. With Diogo one side, Alison the other and Alexander taking her by the hand, they helped her mother from one car to the other. Alison leaned towards the dashboard, started her car's engine and turned up the heater.

'Soon be warm mum, just having a quick word with Alexander'

Alison's mother made no reply, content to just sit in her seat her eyes staring off into the night sky.

'Thank you for all you've done for us tonight Alexander, I don't pretend to know what is was but somehow I feel some great weight has been lifted something ugly destroyed...'

As she spoke her eyes were drawn to the boot of the Volvo, she had seen the two men put the bag into it before they left the cottage. A quick glance at her mother and she was speaking again.

'It was the painting wasn't it, the painting had a '*dark essence*' didn't it, hasn't it?'

Alexander took her eyes into his and put a hand on each of her shoulders, when he spoke it was with a warming smile. 'You, nor your mother need fear it any longer, this 'dark essence' now belongs to someone else, someone called Concetta'

The two men drove into the night and back to Goldworthy Street, Reading in total silence.

Part Five

He had just placed the brass clock on the wooden counter and was reaching in his pocket for his pocket watch when door bell chimed and he felt the presence of a person at his back.

'I think you have a bargain there sir, it'll shine up nicely and keeps good time for its considerable age, I will wrap it for you.'

 From the shop's doorway Alesandro watched his mother carefully fold tissue paper around the clock, slide it into a paper bag and take the proffered note from the customer. As the man

turned to face him Alesandro tried his best to return a smile as he held the door open, no smile reached his lips. The door bell chimed once again and save for Alesandro and his mother the shop was empty. For a long while Concetta studied her son's face and he was well aware read far more from it than he would have wished. And then she was speaking, her voice a low conspirator's whisper.

'I see you have had a fruitful night my son and the female, the Miss Cleaver was she as I...'

She paused and did not finish her sentence, distracted now her eyes were intent on the familiar leather bag as her son raised it to place it onto the wooden counter between them.

'And Diogo is now at his home?'

' I believe he is' replied Alesandro.

Concetta reached for the bag and dragged it towards herself, with one hand she gently pulled apart its drawstring, she placed her other inside and gripped the picture by the edge of it's frame. For a fleeting second Alesandro hoped against hope his mother was going to take her hand empty from the bag's dark interior but all of sudden the object slid from it into the shadowed light of the shop, *what else could he have possibly expected, the painting was in the bag and he knew it?* Concetta was startled by the fleeting look she caught in her son's eyes as the painting emerged...she had only seen it once before in those blue eyes of his..he was a small child and the cornered

black rat in the barn leapt onto his bare arm and bit him to the bone.

--- --- --- --- ---

'You have it in your blood Alesandro, your inheritance handed down from my mother and father to me and their parents to them and so on from time immemorial. The people said it was written that the devil could not demand all he desired without condition, without exception - we are that condition Alesandro, and for now we are that exception. The people spoke of the devil demanding the evil of the 'dark essence' to be his and his alone. The people said it was not to be, it could not be, the devil could not demand as much. Today we are the custodians of those words. Alesandro, you cannot be influenced by this powerful 'dark essence' you have it in yourself to combat it, to withstand its omnipotence, to deflect its evil...It is written Alesandro, it is written, for now we are that condition, that exception.'

With his mother's words of so many years ago echoing in his mind in the tiny upstairs room of the shop Alesandro stood staring at the new addition to the many varied objects that crowded together in its shadows. One took his eye above all the others and filled him with a trepidation that was wholly alien to him. The painting now hanging on the wall amid them all...the one taken from Ivy Cottage. The one that gave out a certain 'dark essence' that shook him to the core.

--- --- --- --- ---

The large featureless building was only a short distance from 'Concetta's Antiques and Curios' a walk-able distance even for an elderly lady who needed a cane to keep her balance and rest her weight on periodically. She was grateful the street lights were on even though it was still only the twilight start to the nights coming. Concetta had absolutely no fear of anything the dark could hold for her but her eyesight was not what it once was. He was home, she was relieved to see, the light from his room shone from curtainless windows four storeys up. By the time she'd negotiated the eight flights of stairs Concetta's lungs were painful in her chest and her legs and hips ached. Her knock on his door echoed loudly down the empty concrete stairwell from whence she came. When Diogo opened his door to her and ushered her in he did it with not the merest hint of surprise on his face, it was almost as if he'd been expecting her, *maybe he had* .

'Concetta, come in, come in, how nice to see you, let me take your shawl, please take a seat'

Concetta let Diogo take the shawl from her shoulders and made her way silently to one of the armchairs, behind her Diogo closed the door but not before taking a sweeping look into the darkened stairwell. The room was sparsely furnished, two mismatched arm chairs, a large wooden table surrounded by three wooden chairs, again mismatched, and a huge old TV standing on what looked like an upturned packing crate. The plain dirty white walls were adorned with pictures of Portuguese landscapes and portraits of Portuguese face's all

smiling in the Portuguese sunshine. In one corner a large colourful but paint peeled statue of Our Lady, arms down at her sides holding her blue mantle splayed out her eyes lowered and unreadable. If Concetta had crossed herself on entry to the room Diogo hadn't seen her do it.

'A little Poncha Senhora Constantine ?'

Concetta gave Diogo a wan smile as she answered.

'I will take a small drink with you Diogo and please call me by my name, we have been friends a long time'

Diogo returned her smile, stood and made his way through a small doorway partially obscured by colourful strings of hanging beads. Concetta sat listening to the pop of a cork and the clink of glasses, she spoke to the beads..

'It is a beautiful painting yes, the colours so vibrant and strangely alive?'

It was obvious to both of them which painting she was referring to. Diogo returned with two glasses both filled, he handed one to Concetta as he sat down on one of the wooden chairs facing hers. The small Portuguese man's reply was hesitant, guarded.

'I did not see it clearly at the time, Senhora, the room was dark because our torch had ceased with its light and...'He paused, Concetta eyes were fixed on his, her drink clutched tightly in her tightly veined fist.

'It was quick that I got... we got the painting into the *bolsa*....the

bag, it was quick I did it, Alexander, he step back'

Diogo tore his eyes from Concetta and stole a look into the corner at the statue of Our Lady, who he never doubted would be listening to his every word.

'You must call me Concetta, Diogo, we are *compagni* are we not, we have known each other for a long time have we not?'

Diogo nodded his head in passive agreement, took a large gulp from his poncha and swallowed hard. The room became silent, the only sound a dull chime from a clock that until then had been invisible on the only shelf on a wall. Concetta broke the silence....

'It is of interest to me Diogo.... what happened that night in the house of Signora Cleaver, and I want to know all, Alexander has been very quiet since, *not himself?*'

Diogo took a swig from a half empty glass of poncha looking in turn at Concetta and Our Lady, he gestured towards Concetta's untouched glass, she shook her head, he disappeared for a few seconds behind the beads and reappeared with his own glass replenished. He sat, took a deep breath and began.

And a deeply trouble Concetta listened.

Part Six

The handwritten letter arrived six days later, it was as all the others, more instruction than request. It gave date, time and place of rendezvous, description of destination and an amount of money that had been estimated for any required necessities, rooms would be available if required for overnight stays. A Mr Michael Patrick had made the impassioned plea and yes, Concetta had studied said 'impassioned plea' and deemed it bona fide in every respect. Diogo was to be at Concetta's Antiques and Curio's to accompany Alexander to Reading Railway Station from whence the journey south west was to commence.

Early morning Dec.12th 2016 Reading Train Station.

The two men sat together in the cold waiting room, Alexander clutching a small suitcase and an empty creased and battered leather bag, already ruing his decision not to take the car, Diogo, a holdall and his coat slung over his arm, he still felt the cold English weather. They had not spoken much on the journey to the station the taxi driver did most of that for them. The train to St. Austell was on time, 11 minutes to wait, from St.Austell it was only a short taxi ride to Gorran Haven and the home of a certain Mr. Michael Patrick. Alexander looked down at his white knuckles on the handle of the leather bag and forced himself to relax his grip.

--- --- --- --- ---

Concetta was standing in the exact spot in the upstairs room of the shop her son had stood only days earlier but it was not the painting she was looking at, for now it was Diogo and Alexander climbing into the taxi on the street below. She waited for the taxi to disappear around the corner and then slipped a liver spotted hand into her heavy cardigan and took out the letter. She would read it again for the tenth time.

Dear Dr. Alesandro...(all the letters addressed for Alesandro were written for her perusal, otherwise they would be addressed to Alexander)....Dear Dr. Alesandro Constantine, my name is Michael Patrick and I am in desperate need of any help you can give me regarding a certain situation I find myself in. I have read many of the articles and thesis you have written, and listened to with great interest your various interviews on radio and in the media. Your researches into ' dark essence' are without precedence. I am totally convinced that you are the only one who can help me. I pray that I do not insult or offend you by offering you financial recompense for your services in this matter but I am a wealthy man and I would gladly divest myself of my entire estate to be rid of the horror that has befallen me.

Dr. Alesandro Constantine I beseech you, help me. Michael Patrick.

Concetta folded the letter and with her eyes now firmly fixed on the painting before her she placed it back in her pocket. She had work to do.

--- --- --- --- ---

The train had reached Newbury before either man spoke but it was always going to be Alexander who broke any silences between the two of them.

'My mother felt the need to converse with you it would appear Diogo?' Diogo had been watching the trees change into buildings and then into fields out of the trains window, he was not expecting such a question from Alexander, he was not expecting *any* questions.

'I followed her Diogo, I followed my mother to your doorstep.' The smaller man just stared opened mouthed, his mind frantically searching for a response. 'She was in your rooms for a considerable time Diogo'

When Diogo managed to speak it was with a nervous caution and guarded words.

'She very concerned about you Alexander, she has a mothers concern about her *filho uniico*, her only son, she feel you tired, she feel you need rest from things, from tudo...everything.'

It wasn't enough and Diogo knew it would not be, Alexander tilted his head slightly and took the little Portuguese man's eyes in his. The train jolted over some points and the carriage rocked but Alexander's stare never faltered, he gestured with hand movements for Diogo to speak on.

'Sua mae, your mother, she tell me that she feel a change in you, a...different mood, she ask if I see this as well'

'And do you?'

Alexander studied Diogo's face, noticed that his fellow passenger could not keep eye contact with him and as he asked his question he watched the man swallow hard before answering...'I say, sua mae, your mother, Alexander he no like painting, he step back at painting, I say I put painting in bolso, Alexander step back, is all I say'

Alexander closed his eyes and lay his head back against his seat, Diogo stared at the face of the man that was his only amigos de verdade, *his real friend* and the carriage became silent once more.

--- --- --- --- ---

Kings Road Auction House Exeter.....August 2013 Lot 203.

It had caught his eye during the morning session as the potential bidders were milling around the auction rooms inspecting the lots. He had handled it, read about it, checked it's authenticity looked it up on line and felt the icy cold exterior that only real marble retains at room temperature. He liked it, it *'spoke to him'* he would definitely bid for it when the auction started in the afternoon. Auctions were his hobby, he was not an expert by any means but he knew what he liked and he

usually got what he liked. Abigail his wife of fifteen years had no interest in the items he bought and not a lot more interest in him. She had her horses and her horsey friends, she wanted for little, Michael's inheritance from his wealthy parents was to thank for that. If her now retired husband was at an auction, he wasn't in her stables. After a light lunch and a quick half at the bar of the pub a few doors up the road Michael Patrick was back in the auction rooms sitting on a tiny wooden seat clutching his bidders numbered card and listening to the auctioneers spiel.

And then Lot 203.

In the corner of the crowded room a young lady in a blue smock was holding up a mottled white statuette, turning slowly from side to side for all the audience to view . The auctioneer commenced. Here we have a fine example of Greek artistry, a likeness of the Greek God of medicine Aesculapius, sculptured in solid marble it is in remarkable condition for its considerable age. I have a lot of interest in the item so I can start the bidding at £2000 . The bidding was fierce the object obviously coveted, after what seemed like an age Michael Patrick's bid of £8575 pounds was the final bid and to his extreme delight the statuette was his. The car sent up a cloud of dust and small stones as its driver brought it to an abrupt stop outside the huge and imposing auction building. The smartly dressed, bearded man exited the vehicle not taking the time to lock it and made his way hurriedly up the few steps into the busy reception area. People were milling past him all making their

way out into the car park, some carrying purchases they had acquired at the sale others empty handed. *He was too late, too damned late.* The bearded man stopped at the big double doors to the auction room turned and made his way back with the crowd towards the car park, his head turning from one person to another, searching them with his eyes for anything they had in their hands or carried in bags. He watched, becoming more and more agitated as their numbers dwindled and the echoes of footfall from the auction room at his back lessened.

'He was too late, it had been sold...or maybe..''

At least he was dressed like an auctioneer, white shirt, waistcoat and black elastic bands holding his shirtsleeves back at his elbows...The bearded man approached him, his throat dry, his heart thumping, he could barely bring himself to ask his question...or relish the curt reply he received..

'Sorry sir you are far too late, Lot 203 the marble statuette of Aesculapius has been sold and sorry I cannot possibly divulge who the fortunate buyer was'

Part Seven

It was a pleasant painting, not a major work of art in any way but nice on the eye. Concetta had taken it down from the wall and lain it carefully on the table, the one she called her 'altar'. As with all of her collected objects she had placed it under a powerful overhead light and with her magnifying glass studied

carefully the paintings surface. A signature of sorts was in the bottom right hand corner but it was no more than a faded and jagged squiggle, the date 1879 was clearer. Starting at the top of the frame she began an intense scrutiny, more out of curiosity than anything else, sometimes she found clues in the objects themselves that revealed the source of what she was searching for, feeling for. The sky had been painted an impossible blue, the grass on the hill too green and the cows that fed on it under magnification just blurred brushstrokes. She then found herself searching abstractly in the blue of the stream that ran between the trees for fish in the water..and her mind wandering...'What was it Diogo had told her when she went to see him, concerned about her son?'

'Alexander stood back from the painting Concetta, he could not raise his arms to take it Concetta, I took the bolso from him and took the painting off the wall Conchetta, I placed the painting in the bolsa, Alexander looked apavorada Concetta...terrified'

This could not be possible, Alexander has engaged with items of considerable 'dark essence' he is immune as I am to...her thoughts drifted away to what lay in hand...

Hurry along Concetta you have much to do... The voice in her head restored her concentration, she now played the magnifying glass on the subjects painted in the foreground. By their dress two females sitting in the long grass and two males standing, all with their backs to her looking at something that was in the invisible distance. Nothing untoward, nothing that could explain.... And then Concetta jumped in her seat almost dropping her magnifying glass. The shop's door bell heralded the arrival of a customer in her shop, the painting would have to wait.

The abode of Mr. M. and Mrs. A. Patrick's Mevagissey...September 2013.

'Have you been buying more trinkets Michael, I really think we have enough cluttering up the house, don't you?

Abigail Patrick had been running a duster over the huge mantelpiece of the open fire, something she did not do often, they had not hired a cleaner only to do the cleaning herself. Anyway it was ploy as good as any other to attract attention to the statuette and she made no attempt to disguise it.

'Michael Patrick's sigh was long and emphasised as he closed the book in his lap and looked up at his wife, she had picked up his latest acquisition and was squinting into its face.

'Its hardly a trinket Abby and its been standing there for a month now, please put it back it was quite expensive'

Ignoring her husband Abigail was now turning the statuette upside down looking for any marks on it's base. Michael Patrick sighed again, he knew it was a waste of time but he'd enlighten her again, hopefully she would not enquire as to how much it actually cost.

'Its a statuette of the Roman God Aesculapius, the god of medicine, it is a thing of great beauty and I happen to like it'.

It was Abigail's time to sigh and as she did so she placed the statuette unceremoniously back in its spot and picked up her cigarettes and lighter that were lying beside it.

'Well I don't' she said 'Its too heavy, cold and I find it strangely scary'

'Michael stood placing his book on the low coffee table before him, he had an incredulous look on his face and when he spoke it was with a questioning tone.

'It's cold and scary Abby, what exactly do you mean by that, cold and scary?'

Abigail made as if to pick up the statuette again but hastily pulled her hand back in as if I the object had leant forward to bite her.

'Look at it' she responded, 'It stands in it's own little shadow on the mantelpiece lauding it over everyone and everything'

Michael opened his mouth to speak but Abigail had more to say.

'When the Peterson's left us the other night Carol says it gave her the creeps, she said that she even dreamt about it when her and Terry went to bed that night, nightmare she said'

Again Michael opened his mouth, again Abigail spoke over him.

'It stares at me Michael, when you are not here it watches me I swear, put it somewhere else or sell it, but get rid of it please, I know its sounds silly but I don't like it in the house.' She was lighting a cigarette as she spoke blowing out smoke between pursed lips. Michael nearly told her then, in the silence that ensued, he nearly told her that he could not move the statuette, he had tried, it would not allow him to, it numbed the muscles in his arms and and at the same time quashed the *want* in his mind. .And then he realised Abigail was staring at him, standing in the silence just staring. And then she sighed a huge sigh..'I'm going to take Chestnut out for a trot' And with that she was gone. In the new silence his wife had left behind her Michael Patrick found himself looking intently at the statuette.

'She will never really understand you will she?' He told it.

--- --- --- --- ----

With an impatient reluctance Concetta tore herself away from her room and the painting awaiting her scrutiny and hurried down to the shop..*'why hadn't she turned the open sign around beforehand she could not fathom...age she thought with a wan smile...*

It was two potential customers, an elderly couple, they both wished Concetta a good morning as they wandered between the shops many shelves, randomly picking up objects and after a brief look putting them down again. Concetta placed both her hands on her counter and composed herself. These people had every right to be in her shop, they were not intruders, then why

did she wish they were gone, why did she feel as if they were delaying her, keeping her from doing something far more pressing.

'Our Malcolm had one of these, it was exactly the same as this one'

The elderly lady was holding up an old barometer, wooden framed, brass and glass faced. Concetta could not recall exactly when Alesandro had brought that particular item to her, but then again Concetta could say the same about most of the objects that had passed through her hands all these years. And then the elderly man was speaking.

'Got some lovely old bits and pieces here Mrs, we could spend all day in here couldn't we June?'

Concetta, standing behind her counter and willing the elderly couple gone, bit her lip then forced herself to reply.

'Thank you' She nearly added *'and now all clean and clear of what brought them to the shop in the first place'* but they would have no idea of her meaning, her admission..she remained silent.

The shop had been Alesandro's suggestion. A way to show the world the face of normality and under this veil carry on their vital work undetected. Buy and sell antiques and curios. The badly troubled items could be visited on by Concetta and then when the 'essence energy' was discovered and destroyed, sold on with the untouched. The shop would be their nucleus.

'I rather like this, what do you think Eric?'

It was June and she was approaching the counter carrying an ornate silver tea pot, her husband following behind her.

'Is it silver?' she asked.

'Silver plated' Concitta's sharp reply was too curt, impolite.. as an apology she quickly smiled and held out her arms..'here, let me wrap it for you'

Concetta heard herself say the words but watched as somebody else's hands wrapped the tea pot before putting it in a bag. She watched as somebody else's hands took the money offered and gave change. She watched as hands held the door open for the elderly couple to step through with their new purchase. And then she watched those same hands as they locked the shops door and turned the open sign to closed. Now she could be alone with the painting, the painting that for some reason she had suddenly felt drawn to. And the hairs on her arms bristled she was certain, because of the cold air that blew in from the closing of the shop's door.

--- --- --- --- ---

Dr. R. Samuels Rooms St. Austall November 2015.

Michael Patrick, sitting upright in a cold metal and plastic chair staring at a blood pressure machine standing redundant on the Doctors desk, words flowing freely from his mouth.

'A voice from somewhere invisible to me 'Call for vir medic this man he is dying, he has the fever, he is dying'. Outside the billowing walls of the tent the wind was howling and gusting, it was a hot dry wind that took with it the moisture from your throat, from your eyes. Again the voice from a soul I could not see, 'Call for vir medic and make haste. And then in the tent at my feet a cauldron, a gurgling cauldron bubbling over with a fire that spat yellow and orange sparks into an already unbearable heat. And then I was not alone, he was there in the tent, vir medic the fires from the cauldron now licking at his long robes turning them black and singeing the skin below. Vir medic lowered his ladle to scoop up the molten liquid spilling drips into the sand of the floor, sending up puffs of dark smoke. Open your mouth, open your mouth, his words filled the tent defying the sound of the wind to enter. Open your mouth, vir medic demanded. I opened what was left of my mouth swallowed and watched my own intestines erupt from a blackened hole that was once my stomach.'

'And you say you have had this dream on more than one occasion ?'

Dr. Samuels was leaning over his notes opened out on his polished wood desk, looking over the top of his glasses, Patrick now silent, shoulders slumped, his sunken eyes red from lack of proper sleep.

'That one and worse but all with the same theme, I am dying, near death and a voice from somewhere calls out for help for me and....what's happening to me doctor why these dreams, what the hell is happening to me?

Dr. Samuels was scribbling something in his notes as he spoke.

'I'd like to refer you to a colleague of mine a ….'

Michael was all of a sudden on his feet, his chair now upended on the floor behind him, his face red and tears welling up in his eye's'

'You're referring me to a fucking shrink aren't you, is that all you can do for me?

He wasn't even aware he had leapt to his feet and slammed both palms of his hands down hard on the doctors desk, Michael slammed the door loudly on his way out. The headache that had began to grow more severe since he had entered the Doctors surgery now his only concern. He had no recollection at all of driving home.

--- --- --- --- ---

'You have not been yourself Michael lately, I hate to see you like this, maybe you do need professional help, did Dr. Samuels make you an appointment?'

Abigail stood up from the sofa and took a step closer to her husband and for one uncomfortable moment Michael thought she was going to take him in her arms and then she was speaking again.

'I can't remember the last time I saw you relaxed, smiling, happy, maybe we need a holiday, somewhere warm, somewhere a long way away from here. I can get Margaret and William to look after the house and Avril and Mel to look after the stables for a week or two, what do you say?

Her husband made no reply, he was staring over her shoulder at the fire place, at the mantelpiece, something on the mantelpiece.

'Are you even listening to me Michael ?'Abigail had raised her voice and was striding purposely towards the drinks cabinet, she followed Michaels gaze as she did so, her eyes came to rest on the statuette...and now her voice was even louder.

'Oh, and by the way I did some research of my own on that lump of stone you seem to be so fixated with all of a sudden.. over eight fucking grand nearer nine wasn't it, nine fucking grand?'

She had taken a single glass and a bottle from the cabinet and was pouring herself a large amount of bourbon...Michael was standing, his eyes never leaving the statuette..his ears now deaf to his wife's ranting.

'Well I think Dr. Samuel's should make you an appointment with a shrink, an appointment with somebody, because sorry darling I don't think you're at all well, I don't think you've been right for a long time'...Abigail paused to take a large gulp of her drink...she tipped her glass towards the mantelpiece spilling some of its golden liquid onto the carpet...and then she was speaking again...

'Its since you brought that stupid thing home with you I'd swear to it, I think the fucking things got into your head, you, sitting there all day talking to it, it isn't normal behaviour Michael, it isn't normal behaviour'

She had gone back to the cabinet and was refilling her glass spilling ash from the cigarette clasped between her thin lips. Michael was watching her closely, her unstable movements implied to him that it was more than her second drink of the day, he fought to keep the tone of his voice steady.

'I don't sit here all day talking to it, don't talk utter rubbish Abby, what the hell makes you say such ridiculous things and lay off the booze, you have been drinking far too much lately, don't think I haven't noticed'

Abigail turned quickly to face her husband, spilling more drink onto the carpet as she did so and swearing under her breath.

'Oh, so it wasn't you I saw kneeling in front of it at 2.am the other morning whispering sweet nothings, telling it you had plans, anything it wanted it could have, you are fucking pathetic Michael and do you know what...?'

Abigail got no further, Michael took a step towards her his fists clenched at his sides his face reddening, his eyes blazing.'What in hell would you see or hear at 2am any morning Abigail you are usually in a drunken stupor, lying flat out on the sofa, mouth wide open, not a pretty sight I assure you'

The glass missed his head by inches and shattered against the wall behind him, Abigail swore again and ran up the stairs slamming their bedroom door behind her.

'I'm calling the police' she screamed, 'you've gone too far this time'

--- --- --- --- ---.

In the sudden silence Michael found himself inexplicitly picking up shards of glass from the carpet, he looked up at the statuette of Aesculapius standing atop the mantelpiece seemingly looking down at him and spoke to it...' 'What am I to do with her?'

It would be a while before he felt the warm blood trickling through his tightly clenched fingers. When the two policemen arrived a short time later in answer to her mobile phone call and threatened to arrest him for the seemingly unprovoked attack Michael was astounded by his wife's change of demeanour. As she came down the stairs she appeared to have calmed down, was even smiling. Almost as if she had regretted making the call at all, an impulse.

'He hasn't been well, his behaviour has become more and more erratic but he was never violent, well never violent until now, he has promised me he will seek further help and in the meantime he is moving into our holiday home in Gorran Haven,

it is not too far away. He has agreed with me it would be for the better.'

'Haven't you Michael darling?'

Michael Patrick nodded duly because that what was asked of him.

'I will not be pressing charges, it was my fault as much as his, sorry if I've wasted your time officers'.

Abigail walked over to Michael and placed an arm on his shoulder smiling sweetly at the impatient looking policemen.

'You can go now officers, we will be fine, just a little tiff that got a bit heated, wasn't it darling?

Michael's smile was on his lips again, his injured hand held tightly behind his back. One of the policemen was speaking....

'We do not want to hear from you again tonight Mr and Mrs Patrick, we have quite enough to do, do I make myself clear?'

(You nearly blew it there, Abby darling, your damned temper nearly wrecked it all for you, calm down, hopefully no harm done this time but keep a check on your fucking temper in future).

Abigail felt much better after her little chat with herself..

The police left the property satisfied that it was a minor *domestic*...Michael was given an informal warning and all was alright with the world. Abigail had gotten herself a fresh glass and was pouring herself another bourbon as she spoke.

'I don't know what came over me Michael darling, sorry, shall I pour you a drink, you look like you could do with one?'

Michael watched as his wife poured him a drink, all that had just happened a blur in his mind, hadn't Abby, just called the police on him, hadn't she just thrown a glass at him....didn't he think just for a split second back there that he wanted nothing more than to kill his dear Abby, take her by her neck and squeeze the air from her body....didn't he imagine vividly himself doing it?

She handed him the glass of bourbon and was speaking again.

'But I do think we need our space darling, I think it would be best for both of us, a few weeks apart to give us both a chance to find ourselves to look carefully at our relationship.'

Michael Patrick could find no argument to his wife's words, another day with her and...Abigail drained her glass, wiped at a tearless eye with the back of her hand and gave him a wan smile. Michael Patrick moved out of the house in under an hour, in total silence Abigail packed some things for him. She had surprised herself though because although she had hated its icy feel and the arrogant aura it seemed to give off she kissed it all the same, it was the first thing she packed, it was the first thing she needed to pack, Michael's statuette of Aesculapius. *She would miss it, she had grown fond of it or it of her she couldn't be sure..she would miss it but to have Michael take it for now was imperative for it's plans to come into fruition. She would have it back in time, it had promised her.*

There were just a handful of cars in the pubs car park, Michael drove into it and slotted his car in between two others. He did not want to be seen and the panic in him had grown to such an extent he could no longer concentrate on his driving. He switched off the engine took out the ignition key and made his way round to the boot. The large suitcase was there along with two carrier bags full of things Abigail had hastily put together for him. No need to open the bags, he lifted them and felt their weight..nothing. He sat the suitcase up on its side and with shaking fingers he pulled the zipper open.

Why would she pack it, it wasn't clothing, it wasn't something you would take with you for a week or two away, there would be no reason for her packing it...but please...'

Michael pulled out shirts, underwear, trousers, and laid them in a crumpled heap on the boots floor his anxiety rising with his blood pressure....

For Christ's sake man why didn't you take it yourself, why didn't you just put it in another carrier bag and...?'

And then his finger tips hit against something solid, something immovable wedged in the sides of the suitcase...

Michael's relief was palatable...so much so that he never gave it a second thought as to why Abigail would even consider putting the statuette in with his luggage in the first place.

And why were his fingers now bleeding so much ??

--- --- --- --- ---

The shop, the house, was at last how she wanted it, empty and quiet, the customers gone with their silver plated teapot and the open sign showing closed to the outside world. Concetta made her way up the stairs and into the room, *her room* and the painting was as she'd left it lying on her 'altar'. She turned on the single overhead light and was mindful of how dark it still was but for what she had to do little light was required. Concetta knelt on all fours and dragged the Ottoman from its place under the 'altar' bringing a fine cloud of dust with it. She ran her gnarled finger tips over its lid and visualised the markings that were etched into it, the identical markings that were tattooed onto the ancient leather bag Alesandro and Diogo were sure to always carry at their sides. Concetta carefully raised the lid of the Ottoman, the hinges were rusted and fragile and as she did inhaled hungrily its pungent but familiar scent. When fully opened her hands searched its black interior until the rough texture of Hessian fabric scratched against the thin skin of her bony knuckles, she gripped it and lifted it out. Now with a creaking of her knees and a groan escaping her lips she struggled to stand and as she did she unravelled the material to lay it flat over the paintings surface.

It started as a low murmur, an involuntary sound issuing from deep in her throat. Concetta's hands were moving in concentric anticlockwise circles just above the Hessians surface and after a

long while and as the room darkened she tilted her head back and the sound became a high pitched lilt. The sanskrit mantra emanating from her open mouth whisked her mind and soul a thousand years away to a place and time she had visited on many occasions before. A place of healing and peace, a place never to be visited by evil.

And it was her desire that the hostile 'dark essence' that had permeated the painting's solid form would indeed obey her demands and follow her there. Concetta leant forward and lay her forehead gently on her 'altar' at the side of the painting, she would meditate this way until total exhaustion stole her away.

Conchetta was awakened abruptly from the deep sleep she had fallen into, she raised her head from the 'altar' and rubbed at her eyes with the backs of her hands to clear her blurred vision'

'Do you find any of this at all amusing my dear..?

'Do you find any of this at all amusing my dear...?'

There, the question was in her head again, the question from the leering man in her dream, in the painting. With a shaking hand and tentative fingers Concetta gripped the side of the Hessian and pulled it slowly towards herself revealing bit by bit of the picture underneath it. The man, the man Concetta now knew as Edward was no longer looking as his companions were at something far away from the pictures reaches, no the man called Edward had turned around completely and was staring out of the painting at her. Concetta could not prevent the

startled scream that issued from her lips as she leapt backwards throwing the Hessian haphazardly over the accursed picture as she did so.

'Oh Olivia, pray tell me you jest, can you really say you have never seen such a bird as a Sparrowhawk before?'

'My dear Lizzie, Olivia would be hard pressed to tell a Sparrowhawk, from a , a swan'

Edward placed his hand on his brothers shoulder and both men laughed heartily.

'They tease, my dear Olivia, men can be so boorish, ignore them'

'I do not pay them any mind Lizzie, I grow tired of their infantile mockery, father says they rely on it as a way of disguising their own ignorance'

Edward and Charles were now in fits of laughter, holding their stomachs and feigning howls of guffaws...All at once Edward ceased his laughter and a leering grin spread across his face as he spoke.

--- --- --- --- ---

It was far smaller than he had expected, sitting amid a row of similar terrace cottages down a shared gravel lane. Alexander checked the address with the copy of the letter his mother had given him and reread the salient part of it.

I pray that I do not insult or offend you by offering you financial recompense for your services in this matter but I am a wealthy man and I would gladly divest myself of my entire estate to be rid of the horror that has befallen me.

Still slightly confused as it hardly looked the the abode of '*a wealthy man*' Alexander gestured at Diogo at his side and both men made their way through an already opened wooden gate and up to the buildings front door. It opened before they reached it and a man best described as 'not prepared for visitors' stood before them.

'Thank God it is you, Dr. Alesandro Constantine, it must be, because nobody apart from that bitch of a wife of mine, no-one is aware that I am living here'

Michael Patrick looked back at the cottage he had just emerged from with a look of total disdain on his face..he spoke as if he were ashamed of it and impatient to explain why.

'This is not my normal place of residence of course, merely a summer retreat, here take my card, this is where you would normally reach me if things were of a usual manner'

It was as if the man was addressing a business associate, but as he spoke Alexander noticed he had trouble balancing, was finding it hard to put his words together, and his eyes flitted wildly between them.

Alexander glanced at the card before slipping it into the top pocket of his jacket, it had gold embossed letters and the place name Mevagissey was all he saw before Michael Patrick stood aside and ushered them in, looking up and down the gravel lane before following behind them into the building. Once inside Alexander and Diogo stood motionless in the darkened room, the spectacle before them rendering them both speechless. What presumably had been the cottage's furniture had been piled high in the centre of the room chair upon chair, table upon table, a bonfire awaiting ignition. A TV set upside down, its legs pointing at different angles to the ceiling, it's screen smashed and dripping glass onto what no doubt had once been an expensive carpet, now ripped and shredded. In one corner an aquarium, its sides just splinters, it's former residents no more than daubs of orange stained into the bare wooden floor boards. On one wall a huge crudely painted penis, on another a stick man hanging by his neck from the gallows. The slurred words from somewhere at Alexander's back were carried to him on a wave of breath that reeked of alcohol.

'Welcome to my humble abode Dr. Alesandro Constantine, it is Dr. Cont..' the drunken man paused, staggered against the door jamb, looked at Diogo, shook his head and carried on... 'Thank you both for taking the trouble to come, as I say there is plenty of room at the Inn and plenty of ale in..'

As he spoke he waved his arms about in mid air upsetting his balance further, almost falling he lowered his voice and whispered a conspirators whisper.

'Jealous of course you know, Abby is terribly jealous but you didn't know that did you? No, nobody knows that of course, we don't talk about that do we Aescuplshish.... Ashpell ? He was pointing to something standing in shadows in the corner of the room....he put his hand up to his wet mouth and blew it a saliva laden kiss, his voice was now an almost incomprehensible whisper...'but we are going to remedy that soon aren't we my sweet, aren't we..?' And then with his bloodshot eyes flicking rapidly from Alexander's to Diogo's once more Michael Patrick's entire body convulsed into spasms of insane cackling and he fell to the floor, bone on wood.

Part Eight

The bed was hardly recognisable as a bed, buried under a mass of dirty and crumpled blankets and lilting badly to one side due to a broken leg, it stood covered with empty whisky bottles and beer cans. Alexander and Diogo struggled to drag the semi-conscious body on to it careful not to stumble on the various pieces of debris littering the stained carpet. Once they'd got the inebriated man on the bed Alexander made to open the rooms only sash window, the stale stench was almost overpowering, he looked around to see Diogo staring at the prone figure of Michael Patrick.

The room was becoming increasingly darker

'As the man said Diogo, let's us find more room at the Inn, it will be pointless trying to speak to him tonight.'

Alexander had moved through the darkness and was groping for a light switch, when his hand fell on a door handle, he had found the only other room at the Inn.

--- --- --- --- ---

It had been an incredibly uncomfortable night for them both, a makeshift bed had been made up in the room, but it was just that, a makeshift bed and it had become colder as the darkness of the night spread. Diogo had abandoned it some time in the early hours and was lying under his clothes on the floor. Alexander lay in the darkness on the damp mattress his mind again visiting a painting, a painting with a group of people enjoying a sunny day, but more than that, much more...and when the shadow suddenly fell over him Alexander's eyes flew open. The man standing in the open doorway had flicked on the overhead 40 watt bulb and now Alexander could see him much clearer. He was skeletal with tight skin drawn around shrunken eyes, his crumpled jacket hung on his shoulders and the knot of his was tie was pulled up and hidden under his greying collar. His hair wild, his scalp visible through its greasy strands and at least a weeks growth of a beard etched on his blotchy face. Below the jacket his trousers were equally as crumpled and on his feet he wore socks but no shoes, exactly how he was attired when Alexander and Diogo had put him to bed. By the weak sunlight that now struggled to get into the room through the off white lace curtains Alexander gauged the time at no later than 6am, he raised himself from the bed and reached for his shirt that was draped over the bedstead. The man's voice came to him as a timid prayer, a hope against hope, a last grasp of any form of sanctuary.

'You *are* Dr. Alesandro Constantine are you not? Only forgive me again I remember very little of last night, I remember very little of any night...I, ...oh my God please....what have I become?'

'Yes I am Dr. Alesandro Constantine and this is my great friend Diogo'

Michael either chose to ignore the smaller man now standing at Alexander's side or just failed to see him through his desperation. His eyes were fixed pleadingly on Alexander's as he stepped forward and placed both hands on the Doctor's shoulders. Alexander fought to stop himself from flinching back as the other man's rancid breath assailed him and his ice cold fingers dug into his skin. And then the poor wretch of a man was speaking again....

'You must forgive me my abominable behaviour of last night, I already owe you a wealth of gratitude for just being here, I am at my wits end and I feel that you may be the only man, men, that can help me'.

Part Nine

'What do you mean Michael's moved out, why, when, are you OK?'

Abigail had waited a few days before ringing her mother, she had rehearsed in her head a dozen times what she was going to say to her but when it came to it the script went out the window. *Besides she was missing it, its effect on her to be more precise, her thoughts, her dreams were just not the same...but then her attention was back 'on the now' and the phone call she was making.*

'Mother it has been going on for a while now I just did not want to worry you, Michael, well Michael has not been too well of late.'

'What do you mean not too well, is he sick, is he in hospital Abigail?'

When Mrs. Barbara Raynes called her daughter Abigail and not Abby, Abigail knew she was being serious she would have to watch her words.

'No not sick mother, not in the sick sense...but we both thought it would be for the best mother, best for both of us..if we...'

Abigail got no further, her mother's voice boomed down the receiver..

'Abigail you are not making any sense, none at all, I'm on my way over, I'll be there as soon as I can, don't do anything silly, do you hear me?'

'Yes mother I'll be fine, you've no need to worry'

Abigail held the receiver to her ear long after her mother ended the call a glimmer of a smile playing on her lips, *not long now.*

--- --- --- --- ---

It had all been a dream, a figment of your imagination Concetta, there was no Olivia, no Lizzie, there was no Charles and certainly no Edward who had somehow managed to turn himself around in a painting and....for God's sake pull yourself together....you had fallen asleep during the Sanskrit mantra...your meditation deep, your concentration lapsed...unforgivable...never happened to you before...isn't it that Diogo put the thoughts into your mind for your dreams to toy with...Alexander he step back Concetta...he step back ..Concetta....I put painting in bolsa...Alexander, he step back..he afraid...something not right with painting..

Rational once again, her heart rate normal, her breathing under control, Concetta approached the flat shape lying on the 'altar' under the crumpled Hessian sheet she had hastily thrown back. Without hesitation and to atone for her unexplainable lack of composure Concetta took hold of the rough material and with both hands pulled it up and clear of the painting beneath.

--- --- --- --- ---

'During the hours of darkness I have these terrible nightmares and for hours of the day they revisit me, I cannot ignore them, I cannot avoid them, sometimes I am someone else, someone ancient, someone not of this time or world, I have thoughts that can only be malevolent.'

They had taken chairs from the pile in the centre of the room and were sitting opposite each other. Alexander and Diogo had dressed in their outdoor clothes Michael had made no attempt with his own attire of that same morning.

'I see things, I hear things, people speaking in languages that I have no comprehension of, I am alive and then I am dead and then I am in limbo watching others from somewhere thousands of miles away...I want to kill, I want to maim...I want to do harm to others to make myself happy...'

He had been staring at a jagged tear in the carpet between his feet as he spoke, now Michael Patrick raised his head and looked Alexander with eyes red from weeping and wide with fear.

'What is happening to me Dr. Alesandro, what in hells name is happening to me, am I being visited upon by a *'dark essence' Dr. Alesandro*, that is what you believe isn't it, that is why you answered my letter by being here, isn't that exactly it Dr. Alesandro?' Can you help me Dr....I fear I am losing my mind, please tell me what it is that is doing this to me.'

Alexander was silent for a long moment and then he stood and without speaking made his way into the room where he and Diogo had spent the night, he came back holding a bag in his hands, a very old and creased leather bag. As he walked towards Michael he averted his eyes down and was looking at something behind the man's back.

'I think you have a very good idea yourself Mr. Patrick, I think you've known all along, but such is its powers that you....'

As he spoke Alexander took unhurried steps toward the statuette of Aesculapius standing in shadows on the carpet in the corner of the room pulling open the bags drawstring as he did so. Michael turned his head and followed Alexander's gaze and although his body was frail and sick his voice was full of a threat.

'Do not touch her Dr. Constantine, I forbid you, I warn you, do not touch her, she is mine, no-one else's.'

' Voce quer nossa ajuda ou nao ... you want our help do you not?'

It was Diogo and Alexander was surprised at the smaller man's unusually harsh tone, he had stepped up to Alexander's side, the two men exchanged knowing glances and took another step towards Aesculapius, bag at the ready.

--- --- --- --- ---

'Concetta, Concetta, Lucia was calling for her daughter and her shrill voice silenced immediately the cicada and stirred the fire flies into dancing, it was late, the sun long gone and it was time her bambino was inside' Concetta brought the cold air and thesmell of pine with her as she entered the casa she shared with her mother, her father having died when she was less than a year old.

'Madre, do trees talk, do stones or rocks or the earth speak?'

Lucia looked into her only child's eyes and smiled, Concetta had always asked her strange and sometimes wonderful questions, she would try to answer them all with candour. 'I believe everything talks in its own way il mio bambino, if you have the grace to listen'

Concetta reached for her mothers hands and looked from side to side and then whispered...

'The trees and stones and rocks talk to me madre, but sometimes I wish they

did not, sometimes they say bad things'

Lucia eye's widened slightly and her grip on her daughters hand tightened'

'Do not be afraid of what the trees and all else say to you il mio bambino, they cannot move, they cannot harm you'

And then her daughter spoke again...'Oh I do not fear them madre, they fear me'

--- --- --- --- ---

In the little room in her shop Concetta stood and with the Hessian still tight in her hands and stared down at the painting on her 'altar'. She saw two men standing, two women sitting and they were all without exception looking away at something far out of the pictures reach. If the man called Edward had ever

been looking at her he was not now.

--- --- --- --- ---

About two hours away, the way her mother drove, Bristol was under two hours if the traffic wasn't too bad. Abigail's estimate of her mothers time of arrival was almost minute perfect. The first thing she noticed was the suitcase, it was a good sign, it meant that her mother was planning to stay for more than just the day, they would have time, time to, *'time to work on her'*....

'Poor Abby, my poor, poor Abby'

Barbara Raynes was hardly through the door before she dropped her bags onto the floor and threw her arms around her daughter.

'What has he done to you Abby darling, what has Michael done to you this time?'

With her head buried between her mothers neck and shoulder Abigail allowed herself the smallest of smiles.

Part Ten

It had not sold all the years it had been there and as far as she could remember no-one had shown any interest in it, it was big and took up far too much room against the back wall. Alesandro would admonish her for taking on such a huge task but it would all be worth it once done, besides he did not have to know did he?. It was a Sunday, the shop was closed, the streets empty and she was all alone, what better day to undertake what for her would be such a heavy chore. Concetta had convinced herself, the too tall bookcase had to go, all the other walls were too busy with shelving. The door to the back of the shop had to be propped open, she searched the shelves and found the wooden

wedge they always used. It wasn't until she had donned her gloves and squeezed herself between the edge of the case and it's neighbour a concrete and brass free standing garden sun dial that a disturbing thought entered her mind. '*What if Alesandro had fastened the bookcase to the wall?*'

He hadn't, with a bony hand between the back of it and gloved knuckles against the wall Concetta was relieved to feel movement. It was long and exhausting work but by 'walking' the large piece of furniture inch by inch and going from one end of it to the other Concetta finally got it to the door. Once there she laid it onto it's side and dragged it out and into the walled

and long grassed garden where she allowed it to topple onto its back. Later she would pack it's shelves with paper pour over a liberal amount of paraffin and put a match to it. But for now she had a painting to hang in the pale shadow on the wall left by a too tall bookcase and somewhere she hoped her son would not see or more importantly sense it.

--- --- --- --- ---

No, she wouldn't freshen up her make up, change the dress she had worn all day, she had made those decisions long before her mother had unpacked the few things she had brought with her and settled into her nightwear. The spare bedroom was one of three and unlike the others it was on the ground floor, Michael had often said it was going to be his office but he never got round to making it so. Barbara Raynes was just leaving that room when her daughter's voice rang out from the kitchen.

'Drink mum? Dinner will be a while yet'

Barbara was very aware at how unkempt and tired her daughter looked but despite that fact she marvelled at how she managed to sound so upbeat, but weren't all the Raynes family made of stern stuff, she would have a nice evening alone with Abby and console her when the tears came.

'That would be lovely' she heard herself respond to the offer of the drink. The lasagne was delicious, the tiramisu divine and the wine was still flowing, it was not until all the dishes were loaded into the dishwasher that either woman mentioned Michael,

when Abigail finally did Barbara was stunned and it would not be for the last time that evening.

'I don't think Michael is fully aware of it mother but as far as I am concerned we are finished, I just can't take his strange behaviour any more' Barbara quickly lowered the glass she was just about to take a sip from, placed it back on the table and reached for her daughter's hands, she held them in her own and looked into the young lady's eyes.

'Oh, Abby, darling Abby surely things aren't that bad, what do you mean strange behaviour? I know Michael can be....' She didn't get to finish her sentence, Abigail pulled her hands away sharply and surprised her mother by the tone of her voice.

'You don't know Michael at all mother, nobody knows Michael the way I do, you never knew him at all really'.

Before Barbara could respond in any way Abigail grabbed her own glass, took a quick gulp and gave out a short humourless laugh, spraying wine from her lips as she spoke.

'Michael is ill mother, has been for quite a while now and I have found it harder and harder to live with, we argue constantly and he often says spiteful things like he is going to divorce me and give all his money to charity'. Barbara sat in her chair speechless, she had sensed at times her daughter and son-in-law had had their disputes but were not all marriages like that, her and her late husband Geoffrey did not always see eye to eye did they?.....But...

'He attacked me mother, did I tell you that, he threatened to kill me, I had to call the police, they said because no actual physical harm had been done they would only caution him.'

Barbara's breath caught in her throat, her words came out as a series of short exclamations and tears welled up in her eyes. 'He threatened you? He threatened to kill you? Surely not....'

'Oh my God Abby, you poor....'

Abigail had by no means finished, things were going well.. she wiped at her dry eyes with the back of her hand and reached for her cigarettes.

'He calls me names, he spits in my drinks, he cuts up my clothes, oh I know he can't help himself because of his illness but I just cannot bear it any longer' Abigail paused waiting for her mother to say something, when she was sure she still had her full concentration she lit up a cigarette and continued...

'And that's another thing, Michael is mad mother, Michael is going insane as I said, he must be mildly schizophrenic'.

'Schizophrenic!' Barbara almost screamed the word.

Abigail was pouring more wine, offering her mother more, the older lady tried to decline by placing her hand over her own glass but Abigail moved it aside and poured it any way, Barbara, catching her daughters eyes, spoke in soft tones...

'Why haven't you spoken about any of this before Abby, we, I, could have done something about it earlier maybe got help for

him, for you, why didn't you..?'

Abigail was quick in her reply her mother was asking too many pertinent questions...

'Oh we have got help for him now, Dr. Samuels referred him to a psychiatrist, he was the one that suggested Michael move away for a few weeks, he said he was under strain but for the life of me I can't think of any strain that Michael was under.'

Again all Barbara could offer was a 'Oh my God! Poor Abby, poor, poor Abby'

It was time, Abigail was where she wanted to be, she took a large gulp of wine then replenished her half empty glass before speaking, she felt she could even work up some tears if she really tried.

'But you can see for yourself tomorrow mother, I thought we could give him a little surprise and both go down to Gorran

Haven and visit the poor man but be warned he's changed a lot since you last saw him.'

And then as if a curtain had fallen Abigail Patrick was talking about the hoards of tourists in Cornwall and what a nuisance they were. In the room that was once intended to be Michael's office Barbara Raynes hardly slept at all that night, the more she tried to remember any of the conversation she had with her daughter that evening the more the alcohol distorted it. And above all a feeling of deep anxiety prevailed.

--- --- --- --- ---

Before anyone had a chance to speak or move, the door bell of the little cottage rang a jaunty little tune from the hallway....apart from raising his eyebrows at the sound Michael made no move to answer it, so Alexander lowered the bag he was holding and motioned with a nod of his head for Diogo to do so.

'And who the hell are you, what are you doing in my house?'

The loud female voice carried easily into the room where Michael and Alexander still stood and both men turned their heads just as it's owner strode in with a sheepish looking Diogo in her immediate wake. Alexander put the leather bag down on the stained carpet and surreptitiously kicked it towards the pile of furniture as Abigail Patrick appeared in the doorway. For what seemed an age she stood transfixed by the sight before, her eyes wide, her mouth opening and closing her fingers tightly gripping the straps of her bag hanging over her shoulders until she finally found her voice...

'Oh my God Michael what has happened here, have we been burgled, have vandals broken in?' And as an afterthought she added 'Are you ok you look terrible?'

The cottages furniture piled up broken seemingly abandoned, the crudely drawn penis and hanging stick man covering the once pristine walls and a stranger standing at her husband's shoulder, a stranger whose eyes stayed on hers for far too long.

'Who are these men Michael and I ask again what the hell are they doing here?'

'They are helping me Abby, they are helping me, I sent for them, this is...'

Michael's words were barely out of his mouth when the sound of the front door closing at Diogo's back caught all but Abigail by surprise.

'My God Abby what in the world has happened here?'

Mrs. Barbara Raynes shouldered passed Diogo giving him a quizzical look as she did so and made her way to her daughter's side before repeating...

'What in the world has happened here?'

'There, now see what you've done Edward, you have frightened the poor lady with your juvenile behaviour, I truly believe an apology is in order'

'I fear Lizzie is right in what she says Edward old boy, now get down on your knees and... as he spoke Charles was walking back from the stream waving a long piece of sturdy bulrush in the air as if it were a sword, Edward bit his lip in an effort to stifle another bout of guffawing. Olivia was struggling to stand up brushing loose grass from her heavy skirts as she spoke.

'Oh why can't you two grow up, must you act like buffoons all the time?'

That was it, Edward could longer hold in his laughter and in unison with Charles let both youths let rip. Lizzie raised her voice to be heard over the clamour...'Aren't you satisfied with yourselves already, can you honestly say you are happy to be in this, this dark and dismal place we find ourselves now, had you not frightened that lovely lady we would not...'

The pale light from the moon seeping through her bedroom window told her it was not too many hours past midnight. Concetta was out from under the covers of her bed and walking barefoot on her bedroom carpet towards the door in an instant. The stairway to the shops lower interior was pitch black but Concetta's footfalls were confident and determined with the dream still vivid and coherent in her mind driving her forward. Grateful for the light now shining through the shops large but dirty window she made her way to the door leading to the garden and was instantly aware due to a rush of cold air that she had left it propped open, she retrieved the wedge and closed it. Once Concetta had the painting safely in her hands all would be well, she would take it from the dark and dismal place on the wall, she would put it back where it belonged, where it demanded to be.

--- --- --- --- ---

Dr. Alexander Constantine watched the irate woman snatch the phone from her bag and snap it open, Michael, with no comprehension at all of what was happening could do no more than stand, his mouth wide open spittle dribbling from his lips.

He seemed to have deteriorated rapidly in such a short space of time, a wild look in his wide eyes.

'Have you come to take me home Abby, I'd like to go home now please, we'd like to go home wouldn't we Aesculapius?'

Abigail ignored her husband completely and turned towards Alexander the phone now held out in front of her...

'Leave immediately and take your little friend with you or I will have the police deal with you, this is my house and he is my husband, you have no right to be here.' Alexander bent down retrieved his bag from where he had kicked it, took one last look at the statuette still standing in the corner and he and

Diogo made towards the cottage's front door. He paused to look back at Abigail and spoke...

'I can help you Mrs. Patrick, I can help you both, you have an item in your possession that has strong 'essence energies' they are affecting Mr. Patrick and I believe they are affecting you also'

Abigail let out a loud humourless laugh, when she spoke her voice was steadier as she fought to regain her composure..

'What the hell are you talking about are you completely mad, are you one of those religious freaks that...?'

Alexander took a step closer to the young woman now holding the phone closer to her mouth ready to speak into it.

'We are here because your husband requested us to be so, we are here because he implored we help him'

Another laugh from Abigail another one that drew her mothers attention because it sounded nothing like her own daughter's. Alexander was speaking again, walking towards Abigail holding an old leather bag up in his hands.

'Please let us help you, we can if only you let us..we understand his problems we can..'

Abigail's curt response cut the air as her fingers dabbed at the phone's keys. She didn't see the quizzical look her mother gave her as she spoke.

'Get out now, no-one can help us, we do not need your help, I will not tell you again'...

Resigned and more than apprehensive about being questioned by the police Alexander with Diogo close behind strode past mother and daughter, out and onto the gravel drive leaving a distraught Michael Patrick standing at the curtain-less windows hands either side of his head watching them leave through red swollen eyes.

Stunned at what she had just witnessed Barbara stood open mouthed looking at her son-in-laws body silhouetted against the light from the window his shoulders slumped his head bowed. At the other side of the room Abigail had replaced her mobile phone and was walking slowly towards her husband, her voice soft, calming, her arms raised to embrace him.

'There, there, darling it's all over now those worthless men have gone and I am here to take care of you.'

Michael turned away from the window towards his wife and buried his head into her open arms whimpering as if he were a child, Barbara looked on an uncomfortable feeling of nausea building up in her stomach, Abigail was speaking again...to her this time..

'Mother, let me take you out to the car, Michael and I will have a little chat and I will be right back out I promise, just a few minutes.'

Barbara Raynes was more than happy to comply, it had all been too much for her, the thought of a few minutes alone to be able to get her thoughts together seemed like really good idea...and besides she was now beginning to realise, Abby was right, her son-in-law was definitely unwell.

Abigail whispered a few words to Michael and then mother and daughter walked from the cottage arm-in -arm to the car.

--- --- --- --- ---

'You will be alright alone with him won't you Abby?'

Barbara asked as Abigail opened the cars passenger door for her.

'Don't worry mother, I know exactly how to handle Michael.'

Abigail smiled as she spoke and closed the car door...

Barbara's nausea grew, the smile just didn't belong there. She could hear Michael sobbing even as she neared the cottage's front door, a quick glance behind and she saw her mother had taken her make up from her bag and was touching up her face using the car's visor. She would have to hurry. Clutching the strap to her shoulder bag Abigail made her way back to the front door.

'I knew you would come back for me Abby, I knew you would, we can work all this out'

Michael was standing before her his eyes sunken and red from weeping, Abigail looked at him horrified and although she couldn't quite comprehend it amused at the same time. Isn't this just as she wanted it?'

Without pausing Abigail pushed her way passed Michael's emaciated figure and made straight for the object she had come back for relieved to see it still standing in its spot in the shadows in the corner.

'When he followed his wife's gaze Michaels scream was piercing and his voice had taken on a strange and frightening tone, his demeanour once of pleading now all of a sudden one of threat.

'Do not touch her Abigail, she is mine, I warned Dr. Constantine and now I warn you.'

In an instant the heavy marble statuette was in her hands, Abigail swung it out in a wide arc and struck the side of

Michaels head making contact with his left temple, his legs buckled under him and he fell an unconscious heap to the floor. It took all her strength but Abigail managed to drag the prone corpse of her late husband to the base of the stack of furniture and lay his body against it. Now with the figure of Aesculapius safely in her bag Abigail felt in her hand bag for her lighter flicked it alight and touched it to the bottom of the crudely assembled but convenient pyre, hurried steps took her from the cottage to her car parked outside.

--- --- --- --- ---

No sooner had Abigail settled in her seat than Barbara let loose a barrage of pent up questions.

'What was all that about Abby, what were those men saying, why does Michael need their help, more importantly why do they think *you* need their help, what is going on, I'm your mother I deserve to know, I worry about you and Michael darling.'

Barbara had turned in her seat to face her daughter, tears welling up in her eyes. Abigail held her voice steady and placed a hand on her mothers quivering shoulder.

'Michael is not well mother, I told you that, he has this strange idea that, well that something or someone wants to harm him, he has been reading and watching all sorts of nonsense and...'

Barbara could not help herself interrupting..

'But what's all that got to do with those strange men in your cottage..'

It was Abigail turn to interrupt her mother.

'I honestly don't know, but I think I have scared them off.'

Barbara turned in her seat to stare back at the cottage hoping to see Michael at the door or at least looking through the curtains, he was at neither.

For a few seconds an awkward silence filled the car and then Barbara spoke in a softer tone.

'Has Michael calmed down at all Abby?

Abigail clipped on her seat belt and started the engine...

'Yes mother', she answered ' I have made sure that he is a lot calmer now'

Her smile threatening to manifest itself into full out and out laughter, she checked her mirror before pulling off.

--- --- --- --- ---

It took about fifteen minutes before they found what they had hoped to find. The cafe was small with only half its tables occupied and to Alexander's relief the one at the window was vacant, he motioned Diogo to sit at it and went to the counter to order coffee. Alexander's intuition told him that the two women would not stay at the house for too long alone with Michael, on leaving he had noted their car parked on the gravel driveway, a pale blue Ford Focus and he and Diogo watched for it as they drunk their coffee. Abigail and her mother would have to come this way, the only reasonable way out of Gorran Haven and in less than fifteen minutes they did precisely that. Alexander and Diogo waited a further five minutes just to be on the safe side, finished their coffees and made their way out of the cafe to the sound of a fire appliance's two tones coming from the street outside. The two men instinctively hastened their step back the way they had come only minutes earlier and were stunned by the sight that befell them when they reached the cottage. Black smoke billowed out from the buildings windows and door, the air was filled with the acrid smell of burning wood and plastic. A small crowd had gathered outside on the gravel road held back by a couple of hi viz clad policemen. The firemen were busy rolling out the hoses and erecting ladders behind a barrier of hastily erected red and white tape well away from the heat and smoke. Alexander and Diogo stood transfixed as seconds later two fireman in breathing apparatus carrying what was obviously a body on a stretcher, emerged from the cottage a cloud of smoke following their movements.

'From what I' been told 'parently some crazy ole bloke 'ad built a bonfire in there a few days ago, our Daisy sed she'd seen it through the window...not snoopin mind, my Daisy ain't one fer snoopin...well, looks like now ee lit don't it?'

The old man with the old dog on a rope lead had sidled up to Alexander's side and was shouting over the sound of the jetting

hoses before being interrupted by an explosion that took half the buildings roof off.

--- --- --- --- ---

Apart from Abigail asking her to wait in the car for a few minutes while she popped back into the cottage, for Barbara the car journey back was uneventful and silent. For their own reasons neither women willing to start a conversation until they were back in the privacy of the house in Mevagissey.

Once they were there Abby made her way straight to the drinks cabinet, it was early afternoon and well past the time for her first, besides after all that had transpired she was entitled wasn't she? Barbara sat down on the large leather Chesterfield sipping at the cappuccino she had poured herself, Abigail stood at one of the windows looking down at the harbour a hundred feet below nursing her oversized glass of bourbon. Abigail winced when she heard her mother say 'Isn't it a bit early darling?' but made no reply and then as if to justify her actions she turned to face her, put on a huge smile and made as if to toast her with her glass. Barbara did not respond as Abigail had hoped instead she frowned at her and made a 'tut tutting' noise under her breath.

'I'm sorry mother but it has really been hard for me lately, Michael has been impossible to live with, he has changed mother, you saw him, what do you think? He looks terrible doesn't he and what those strange men are doing with him in our....?'

Barbara interrupted her daughter but even she felt her explanation flimsy for some reason...'One is a Doctor, Abby, Michael told you he was and is there to help him..'

'And the other one, the short one who didn't say a word all the time we were there, what was his job, to take notes ?'

Abigail was pleased by the sound of sarcasm in her own voice, she took a large gulp of her bourbon to congratulate herself.

Barbara stood up briskly to put her empty cup on the ornate glass coffee table and her anger at her daughters behaviour was more than evident in her raised voice.

'There really is no need to take that tone with me Abigail and you are drinking and smoking far too much.'

Ignoring her mother completely Abby emptied her glass in one go as if to spite her and started unsteadily back to the drinks cabinet, when she got to it she started pouring herself another drink and paused, the bottle neck hovering precariously in mid air. She turned to face her mother an exaggerated look of intrigue on her face and her voice full of suppressed amusement.

'I've just been thinking mother, why do you think that crazy Michael stacked up all the furniture into a big pile and painted that stick man on the gallows, do you think he was going to hang himself, and what about the huge cock...? That was all Abigail could say, the laughter burst from her on a spray of spittle, and she splashed the whisky all over the hand holding the glass. Barbara was at her daughters side in an instant, she made a grab for the glass but Abigail twisted her body to one side, raised her hand and held it over her mothers head.

'No you don't mummy, no you don't'

Abigail's manic laughter seemed to be uncontrollable, she staggered back into cabinet almost knocking it over, sending bottles and glasses crashing to the floor. Barbara stood back, grasped her daughters upper arm, pulled her around and slapped her as hard as she could across the face. The laughter ceased immediately but the wide grin stayed on Abigail's reddening face, she stared at her mother without speaking for what seemed like an age with something like hatred in her eyes...

'I need a drink' She finally said as she continued to fill her glass.

For a moment Barbara had no idea what to do, what to say, she stood open mouthed her hand stinging from slapping her daughter and the sensation of tears welling up in her eyes.

'I'm sorry Abby, I'm so sorry, I should not have done that'

Again Abigail ignored her mothers words and acted as if nothing had happened, she offered the bourbon bottle towards her and frowned as she watched her shaking her head no in answer. Abigail took another gulp of her drink and walked over towards the sofa with it, she sat, patted the cushion next to her and gestured to her mother to sit beside her, Barbara followed as if she were a sheep obeying the sheep dog. With one hand

draped over the Chesterfield's side, the other gripping her whisky tightly and her voice slurring, she turned to face her mother...

'Let me tell you about Michael mother shall I? Let me fill you in as they say'

Without waiting for her mother's reply Abigail lit up a cigarette and began. 'Michael has got himself another woman, there I've said it, he has been seeing her for a while now, they share things and talk behind my back, they don't know I know but I do.'

Barbara made as if to place her arm over her daughter's shoulder, she wanted to console her, comfort her, Abigail put her hands between them with her palms facing out to dissuade her. And then she was talking again.

'Sometimes I could hear them late at night, they whispered and thought I couldn't hear them but I could, I could hear every word, they tried so hard to be quiet'.

As if to emphasise her words Abigail childishly placed her index finger upright and tight against her pursed lips. 'Shhh!'

'Abby darling' Barbara made as if to turn and face Abigail but she motioned with her hands for her not to move as she herself stood up. Barbara sat tensely on the edge of her seat and watched incredulous as her daughter made her way across to the drinks cabinet, speaking to the room as she did so.

'Do you know something funny mummy, shall I tell you a secret, Michael's secret?'

Abigail had reached and taken the bottle of bourbon from the cabinet, she was refilling her glass once again as she spoke and she stubbed out her cigarette with heavy little stabs into the ashtray.

--- --- --- --- ---

'Race you down to the stream and back, first one there grabs another bulrush brings it back here and wins the challenge.'

Edward playfully punched his brother's arm and without waiting for an answer started off down the grassy incline towards the trees and the stream that meandered between them.

'Hey, that's not fair you scoundrel you have a good head start on me'

Charles was remonstrating loudly as he started after Edward almost stumbling in his efforts to catch up with his sibling, both young men making loud and ungentlemanly whooping noises as they stumbled away on the uneven surface.

'Will they ever grow up? Honestly look at them, school boys in men's breeches'

Lizzie was smiling as she spoke, hand over her eyes as she squinted in the sunlight, watching the two figures as they lurched further away, Olivia now sitting down next to her burst

into giggles.

'Boys never grow up surely you know that my dear sister' *she responded and then abruptly her giggling ceased, she was looking in the other direction, standing on tiptoe to get a better* view, towards an area shaded by the trees and away from the stream.

'Do you see that?'

Now Olivia was pointing, one arm outstretched the other pulling at her sister's wrist gently coaxing Lizzie to her feet.

'Look Lizzie, look, someone is standing under that tree, in the shadows, can you see them?'

Lizzie, now at her siblings shoulder shook her head, try as she might she could only make out the....and then movement, only slight but enough to catch her eye.

'I see them now Olivia, yes I can see...'

The laughter had grown louder with the panting and thudding footfalls, another sound, that of bulrush stems swishing through the air. Charles feigned crashing to the ground as if pole-axed, his brother landing on top of him issuing loud grunts and guffaws.

'Edward, Charles, stop being so annoyingly childish, be sensible for just one moment if you can and come over here'.

She was the eldest of the family and when Olivia used her

'stern' voice the two brothers usually took it seriously, but it was also the look on her face that silenced them this time. They both stood and brushed grass and dirt from their clothing making their way toward the young ladies and looking intermittently at where they saw Olivia was still pointing. Edward was first to slow his rapid panting enough to speak.

'Sorry old girl I can't see a blessed thing apart from trees and the damnable sunshine'

Charles, Edward and Lizzie were now turning their heads to look at Olivia and then in turn towards where she was now gesturing clearly with a degree of irritability. Then the tiny figure moved, even from a distance it was seen to turn, now it was facing them and for all to see, it was slowly approaching. And then it was Lizzie again and her voice rang out with undisguised glee.

'It is Concetta, the lady who so much wants to be with us'

Edward glanced at his brother and then returned his gaze to the approaching figure, he spoke to no-one in particular..'She seems to have her wish'

--- --- --- --- ---

It was the silence that struck her first, a silence that was so total she could actually feel it, see it. And then the sun on her skin, warm and constant. She could not move but she was moving, climbing steadily upwards on legs that were not hers. Now in the film that was showing before her eyes two figures

appeared, in and out of her sight she watched as their mouths opened and closed, they were running but running nowhere into a nothing far away from her. In her peripheral more *figures, two more figures, their eyes looking down at her, smiling mouths again opening and closing but with no sound. At last Concetta was there, amongst them, staring up at the skies, azure with large cumulus clouds frozen in place, no longer drifting, no longer blown. In the distant background a green bush covered hill rising from fields dotted with the blurred forms of long forgotten cows, heads down silently feeding and ignoring all else as they had been doing for decades. Between a bunched group of gnarled and twisted trees a brook's faint blue and silver waters held still in its silent babbling with the capture of time. Concetta was with*

them and all else gone…..and then the sound, the unearthly scream shattering the silence like a steel hammer smashing through glass....and she was awake, her body bathed in sweat, awoken by her own anguished cry. Concetta for the first time in her life felt fear, true fear. She needed her son, Alesandro, the day she always dreaded may have finally dawned.

Part Eleven

'You cannot possibly stay here on your own Abby darling, you've been under considerable stress and I am worried about you, come back with me darling I'm sure you'll feel much better after a time'

They were in the immaculate kitchen of the house in Mevagissey, mother and daughter sitting opposite each other, Barbara pretending not to see yet another glass of the golden liquid in her daughter's hand.

'Why don't you darling, come back with me, spend a few days away from here, just us two, as I say I'm sure it will do you good'

Abigail had been staring off into space, Barbara was not sure if her daughter had listened to a word of what she had just said and then realised she hadn't when the younger woman finally spoke...

'Do you know what Michael told me? He told me that he didn't want me to have any of his money, our money, Michael told me that he'd rather kill me than let me get *'my dirty little tramp hands'* on a single penny.

Abigail took a large gulp of her drink leant forward so as to gain her mother's eyes, fleetingly glanced around the room and then satisfied they were alone whispered...

'I know a lot of things that Michael was planning and I knew what he was doing when he told me he was playing golf or going to another of his fucking... ' Abigail paused, said oops with her hand over her mouth and giggled....

'Didn't mean to swear..meant to say flipping auctions' and then she was giggling again.

Barbara could do no more than sit, the frown on her forehead growing deeper and deeper. Abigail had stood up and was making her unsteady way to the lounge, she came back with two glasses of bourbon placing one in front of her mother as she slumped back onto her seat.

'What was I saying...?' she began but Barbara was quick to interrupt her..

'Come back with me darling, you will feel much better after a good meal and a long hot bath'

Again Abigail, her eyes beginning to glaze over totally ignored her mother, she spilt some of her drink as she raised it to her lips her index finger poised in the air as if making some important point, she was taking a cigarette out of the packet pretending not to see her mothers reproachful looks...

'I knew all about what Michael was planning all along, he didn't fool me fool, no he didn't fool me'

Abigail took two attempts to place the cigarette between her lips and eventually lighting it, she inhaled deeply, eyes closed tight and was hardly aware of letting the rest of them fall from the packet onto the floor.

Barbara's feelings of concern had turned to anger, she was standing, pushing the glass of bourbon on the table away from her as she did so...

'You've had far more whiskey than is good for you my young lady, you are slurring and talking utter nonsense, go and pack some things you are coming home with me...'

Abigail stared opened mouthed at her mother alarmed by the sudden outburst and not quite sure how to respond and then words flew from her mouth before she could stop them carried on a wave of manic giggling ….

'Yes of course, I'm going to pack all my things and to hell with Michael and his fucking money' Abigail paused... 'Oops, sorry there I go, swearing again, naughty girl'

Before Barbara could utter a word Abigail had silenced her giggling and had moved closer to her mother - her voice had become serious.

'I was always coming back to Bristol with you mother, Michael didn't know but Aesculapius did, we had discussed it, we knew what we were doing all along you see' Abigail paused to take another pull from her cigarette and nearly choked on it ...and her words began to flow again...louder.. 'Aesculapius and I planned it all you see...I just left her with him for a while to..to keep him company...' Something in her words made her pause and Abigail let out a strangled laugh before speaking again... 'We are going to be together forever now Aesculapius and I and... *us I should say* ..and do you know what mother?' Abigail had leant forward and taking her mother's eyes in her own she whispered....

'Aesculapius has told me she cannot wait to make your acquaintance mother, she told me she is looking forward to that very much'

Barbara had stopped listening, it had occurred to her that her daughter been obviously taking something, hadn't she read about it in the supplements she so eagerly devoured, yes that was it, Abigail was under the influence of some sort of narcotics and mixed with the copious amount of alcohol she poured down her neck, hardly surprising really when you considered Michael's behaviour and the insane look she saw in his eyes. Mrs. Barbara Raynes would take her daughter home and get her the help she so desperately needed.

And this person' Aesculapius' that Abby kept refering to... she'd certainly have to find out more about her.

--- --- --- --- ---

As another fire appliance arrived at the scene Alexander and Diogo stood mesmerised by the inferno before them, both in total silence, both deep in their own thoughts. It wasn't until the different two tone sounds of an approaching police car reached Alexander's ears that he realised it would be prudent of them to make themselves scarce, he would have no answers for their obvious questions. Alexander had spent his entire life avoiding any type of officialdom the nature of his and his mother s work required the lowest profile possible because if breaking the law was ever deemed necessary neither would balk from doing so. Besides any dalliance on their part would not benefit them in the slightest because the cause of this particular 'dark essence' was no longer available to them, it had been removed and both men were well aware of that fact. They were also well aware that it needed to be found, found before it could perpetrate any more of its evil. With little to be done they made their way to the centre and more densely populated area of 'Gorran Haven' in search of a taxi back to St. Austell and a train to Reading.

--- --- --- --- ---

With her mothers help it took Abigail little time to pack and to make telephone calls to both Mel and Avril, the pair were more than happy to look after the stables and the horses especially when Abigail mentioned the extra money she would pay them. Once on the road back to her home in Bristol with Abigail sitting next to her in the passenger seat flicking from channel to channel on the radio and occasionally singing as if she did not have a care in the world Barbara's curiosity finally got the better of her.

'Abby darling I am a bit confused, in your house in Mevagissey you said Michael didn't know you were going to come back with me but who did you say did know?'

Without taking her hand from the radio's switch or even looking at her motherAbigail's reply was bright, buoyant and immediate'

'Why Aesculapius of course, she knows everything I told you didn't I?'

Her mothers next question went unspoken as Abigail brought the conversation to an abrupt conclusion..

'You want to know what Aesculapius is mother, don't you mother? Don't worry you'll be meeting her soon, now shhh, I like this one'

As she spoke Abigail could picture the statuette packed neatly in the boot of her mother's car along with her clothing and other necessary luggage.

Barbara could not calm the uneasy feeling that was spreading through her stomach, she must have misheard her daughters words...*of course, Abigail is distressed isn't she poor darling ? She has just left her husband for Christ's sake. She is not herself...*

--- --- --- --- ---

Two fire appliances were called to a large house fire on the outskirts of Gorran Haven today. It hasn't been confirmed by police at the scene but it is believed that there was one fatality. The cause of the blaze has yet to be established but suicide has not as yet been ruled out.

Abigail had just refilled her glass when the local news station on the TV made the announcement, she was pleased to see no reaction at all to it on her mothers face, she reached for a cigarette from the packet on the coffee table and sat down. She kept her smile hidden.

'Why don't you give Michael a ring, just to check he is OK, he was in a terrible state when we left wasn't he ? I'm sure...'

The smile that had played on Abigail's lips was gone in an instant and she felt her heartbeat quicken in her chest. Her eyes flew to the TV screen and her brain swimming in alcohol could not tell if the news report had actually finished or was still playing. And then her mother was speaking again...

'No, I suppose it would be best to let a little time pass before you do, you know what they say '*time is a great healer*'

Abigail found herself smiling again and then the smile turned to a little giggling.

Not for the first time today Barbara felt her stomach tightening, she forced herself to ignore it by smiling herself and catching her daughter's eye...as she spoke she stood to make her way into the kitchen for the umpteenth time.

'Now, I bet you feel a lot better darling after your bath, dinner wont be long and a good nights sleep will do you the world of good, I'm so glad you decided to come back with me here for a few weeks Abby, it will do you good and give you time to maybe talk...'

An alarm from the oven cut her off in mid sentence.

'So am I' Was the young lady's loud reply to her mother in the kitchen, as she pulled an old bathrobe over her still warm from the bath body.

'*Weeks*' Abigail whispered under her breath, '*We will have plenty of time and nobody of any consequence knows where I am.*'

--- --- --- --- ---

Damn, she didn't remember the bourbon bottle was empty when she put it back in the cabinet, another wine or two would have to do. The dinner had been filling and even her mother had joined her in a glass of wine, it had been an exhausting day. Abigail looked over at her mother drowsing on the sofa, if she was quiet enough she could get into the kitchen and back without disturbing her, she'd had enough of *(don't you think you've had enough darling?)* all evening.

As the young lady made to stand she lost her balance and fell back against her arm chair making a grunting noise as she did so, Barbara was awake instantly.

'Oh sorry darling, I must of dropped off, are you ok?'

Abigail was attempting to stand up again, the wine bottle in the fridge was beckoning.

'Yes, yes mother I'm fine, why don't you go to bed, you look awfully tired'

Barbara was almost imitating her daughter as she tried to stand but for her it was fatigue not alcohol impeding her movements. As she spoke Abigail was disappearing into the kitchen, she yawned and spoke through the cupped fingers that were now covering her mouth....'I think I will darling...'

'Sweet dreams' mother' Abigail called from the kitchen, 'Sweet dreams'

And although Barbara so wanted to stay up later to talk to her daughter all she felt was an overwhelming desire to close her eyes and sleep.

'Good night darling, see you in the morning' was all she could muster and seconds later she was pulling the sheets over her almost unconscious head. Downstairs in the lounge alone at last Abigail poured herself another drink, retrieved the bag she had surreptitiously placed behind the sofa, took out her beloved statuette and after careful consideration placed it on the middle shelf of the bookcase. She gulped down the rest of her wine, kissed Aesculapius tenderly on the head and made her stumbling way to her allotted bedroom.

--- --- --- --- ---

'Mrs Patrick, Mrs, Abigail Patrick?

She'd been expecting them, she'd been told about the fire, the cottage had been virtually razed to the ground but this would be another matter, another matter completely. Abigail response was immediate..and said with a smile on her lips.

'Yes, I am Abigail Patrick?'

There were two of them, solemn in their dark coloured suits and polished shoes. Abigail liked men to wear nice clothes and polished shoes. It was early afternoon and she'd only just come in from her gardening, the clouds were getting thicker and a smell of rain in the air.

'May we come in?'

He was holding up a card an ID. card Abigail barely glanced at it.?'

The man on the left of the two on her doorstep was speaking and Abigail could not help but notice he had kind eyes, dark brown.

'Oh, forgive me, sorry, please come in, come in'.

Abigail stood aside and gestured with an outspread arm to the open door of the lounge and still smiling said 'Please take a seat'.

'We'd rather stand if you don't mind Mrs Patrick, we have some rather bad news for you I'm afraid, maybe you would you like to sit down yourself?'

'What is it darling, what do these gentlemen want, we know all about the fire, is it about Michael do you think...?'

Barbara had walked into the lounge from the landing, she'd been upstairs doing whatever she did upstairs. It was the second man speaking now, his eyes were blue and he had a nice deep voice, a sleepy voice, Abigail sat down, looking up at her new visitors, Barbara remained where she was standing in the doorway. The man with the brown eyes coughed a little, thought about putting one hand in his pocket and quickly changed his mind and then was talking.

'May I ask who you are madam ?'

He had a good idea who the lady who had just appeared was but he needed to ask anyway.

Abigail answered for her...

'This is my mother Mrs. Barbara Raynes....' she paused and then looking at her mother she continued...'I think you should go back upstairs mother, I think you might find this all rather upsetting'

The two men exchanged puzzled glances but said nothing as without a word the lady in the doorway turned and speaking over her shoulder disappeared up the stairs...'Good day gentlemen'

In the fleeting silence one of the men cleared his throat loudly with the desired effect of once again gaining Abigail's attention.

'I'm afraid the bad news is concerning your husband, Mr. Michael Patrick'.

Abigail shifted in her chair her eyes going from one man to the next, she opened her mouth to speak but 'brown eyes' beat her to it..

'I'm afraid badly burned human remains were found in the building and dental records along with forensic tests prove unequivocally that they were of your husband Mr. Michael Patrick '

Abigail groaned loudly and put her face in her hands...'Oh my God what happened, tell me please what happened...?'

The deep voice replied..

'I am sorry to tell you Mrs. Patrick but all the signs indicate that your husband took his own life'

A silence fell in the room both men waiting for the young lady sitting before them to respond, to react...when she finally did what they heard surprised them both.

'Oh, it was suicide alright, I'm sure it must have been....he wasn't well you know, talk to his doctor, poor Michael'

Abigail her faced still buried in her hands, spoke through her fingers a slight catch in her voice...she did not see the lingering look that passed between the two policemen...and still didn't look up when one of them spoke.

'I'm sorry Mrs. Patrick but we will need speak to you again in due course, just to confirm and clear up a few details, I'm sure you understand'

Again spoken between her fingers...

'Of course, poor Michael, we all knew he wasn't well, but this....'

Abigail had removed her hands and was smiling up at both men in turn...

And then it was brown eyes speaking again...his voice calm.

'I will leave you our card, if there is anything we can do or anyone you would like us to call Mrs. Patrick don't hesitate to...

He got no further, movement at the lounge door took everybody's eyes. Abigail was now standing staring over incredulously at her mother, her voice stern her smile gone.

'I thought I told you to stay upstairs mother, you know you aren't feeling well'

Abigail's mother gave her daughter a little smile, turned and went back upstairs, in turn Abigail smiled at the policemen as they made their way past her to the front door.

--- --- --- --- ---

They had been sitting in the unmarked for a while before either one spoke....

'What the fuck was all that about?'

'You felt it too, I thought I'd imagined it'

'I could have sworn I heard her giggle at least once behind her hands.

'Did we tell her she'd just won the lottery ?'

'I thought she was going to ask me out?'

Brown eyes put the car into drive and started out on the road out of Mevagissy.

The windows needed cleaning and the shops shelving and floors a really good dusting. It was only just after seven in the morning but Concetta found herself wandering around in the semi darkness randomly taking down from the shelving objects that had been *'cleansed'* by her and stored for sale by her. It was something she did occasionally, something she needed to do and on this particular morning she was beginning to realise why. The dream of the night was still with her, its foggy

remnants following her around the shop and all the time refusing to allow her to be completely alone. But it was more than the dream that held influence over her, as if that wasn't enough, it was the low lying, hardly discernible energies that invaded her senses, the energies that seeped into her being, like tiny whisperings, inaudible but still there, the shop and its contents was alive with them, and now she found herself standing in front of the painting, her eyes searching for the slightest movement, the slightest drifting shadow, she could easily imagine it but never quite see it...for the second time in one day Concetta felt fear....*'We are that condition Alesandro and for now we are still that exception.'* She wondered if Alesandro was of the same thoughts...were he and she still *'that condition, were they still the exception ?'*

The answer to that question would explain a lot.

--- --- --- --- ---

The air was cold, the night sky above blacker than black but the myriad of garishly coloured lights that flashed, blue, yellow, green, red, lit up in her eyes and brought vivid colours to her already flushed cheeks. Loud ear thumping music mingled with the laughter and joyful squeals of a thousand milling people assailed her ears so much so that she found herself confusing walking with dancing. The smell of frying hamburgers and onions wafted on the breeze from the large windowed trailer toying with her stomach and taste buds. Discordant voices and half finished sentences abounded...' 'Here try your luck madam, hook a duck...Step this way, win the lady a prize sir...Jump

aboard folks and be taken on a ride that will show you the very stars in the universe..' Her father handed her a huge pink candyfloss that stuck to her nose when she tried to bite into its nothingness and dribbled sticky goo over her tiny clutching fingers. The arms of the Ferris wheel way above her head threw intermittent shadows on the long grass below her feet and the lights chasing the horses around the carousel skipped up and down before her eyes...And then the white faced man with the arching eyebrows, rouged cheeks and bright red nose appeared in front of her as if from nowhere, holding out a bunch of gaily coloured paper flowers that he'd produced from somewhere hidden in his oversized crimson jacket. His black painted upturned mouth was moving but his words were coming from somewhere else far away...He was bending down looking at her, he had singled her out in the crowd he had been waiting for her, searching for her, the little girl in her new velvet green birthday coat.

'Well looky here, lucky little missie, you've won a prize, look everyone, this lovely little missie has won a prize'

She could now clearly see as the man in the crimson jacket bent down to catch her eyes the paint on his face crusty and peeling, the yellow stained pointed teeth in his grinning mouth. He was holding out something, gesturing her to take it with nods of his head at her and the audience of cheering people that had gathered around without her notice...

'She's won a prize' a voice from the throng announced, 'the little missie in the green velvet coat has won a prize'

She stepped forward hesitantly, the crowd closing in behind her, hands on her back coaxing, nudging, their hot exhalations on the bare skin on the nape of her neck under her collar. Another grudging step forward closer, the smell of the white faced man with arching eyebrows and bright red nose, rancid breath filling her senses.'You've won a prize little missie, look, you've won a prize!'

They were cheering all around her people cheering, chanting..

'She's won a prize look, little missie has won a prize'

And as the little girl felt the cold weight of the statuette drop into her outstretched hands all around her was gone, was silent and back to black.

--- --- --- --- ---

It felt strange creeping down her own stairs in her own home but as she made her way down it became easier, Abby's snores told her her daughter was indeed in a heavy alcohol induced sleep. The kitchen door was open and the light from its window sufficient to see her way across to the fridge. Good, plenty of milk for a hot drink. She hadn't seen it on her way to the kitchen but now sitting in her lounge sipping at her hot drink it was all she could see. She could see it because it had never been there before and now it was...and it demanded Barbara's attention, full attention...again.

The headache was as bad as they had been for the last few months and it was a while before her brain recognised the unfamiliarity of her surroundings. Abigail was in the spare bedroom of her mother's house, the one she had slept in as a child. The small clock on the bedside table told her it was 04.15 in subdued green numerals. She lifted her head at a sound that had come from downstairs and winced as pain shot across the backs of her eyes and into her temples. Below stairs Barbara was sitting on her favourite chair in her lounge, looking proudly into the icy cold eyes of her prize....the one she had won at the fair.

'Mevagissey'

Diogo's frown widened but he said nothing, Alexander was holding the small business card Michael Patrick had given him, he had taken from the top pocket of his jacket and was studying it, talking to himself....

'This refers to where Michael Patrick had lived before he moved to the cottage in Gorran Haven, there is a telephone number on here but for obvious reasons that is no good, nobody answered it when I called, Abigail Patrick has since moved to live with her mother, where, we do not know, we will have to go to Mevagissy Diogo, I can see no other way, we need to find the statuette, we need to find Abigail Patrick, and maybe God will smile on us...'

God smiled on them...

It was a tiring drive down to Mevagissy, Diogo not used to the confines of a road vehicle, for most of the journey feigned sleep, Alexander was happy with the silence, he had much to ponder on. Obtaining the Patrick's home address was easy, the local postmaster being of the old school, friendly and helpful and soon Alexander and Diogo found themselves sitting in the car outside the huge and imposing building alert to the fact that its entrance door had just opened and two young women were exiting it engrossed in conversation. It was Mel who gave Alexander her employer's mother's address and phone number in Bristol. She'd had it on a piece of paper in her back pocket, she was intending to call Abigail that night to establish when to expect her back, the horses food was dwindling and she was becoming anxious. Avril just stood quietly a disapproving look on her face at her co-workers blatant and obvious betrayal. *Mrs. Patrick would be furious for sure..didn't she hear her tell the housekeeper not to give her mother's address to anyone ?*

And then Alexander and Diogo were gone, leaving Avril and Mel arguing at the building's doors.

Part Twelve

The room had become noticeably cooler, the shadows deeper and with more substance, the street below gradually quieter of both vehicles and pedestrians. Concetta held her wrist up to the last of the fading light that had managed to infiltrate the dusty window of the shop and through squinting eyes consulted her tiny gold wristwatch. It was getting late, Alesandro would be

home soon she told herself, he had to be. How long she had been sitting, turning her head from one side to the other to search the street for her son, only the muscles in in neck gave any clue, they ached. She had closed the shop when no-one had entered it for over an hour and a half...far later than she would normally turn over the 'Sorry Closed Sign'.

'Go and look at the painting Concetta, go and look at the painting, you will see

it for what it is a mere painting, an inanimate object' she chided herself.

'Go and look at the painting, it cannot harm you, you foolish woman, you who fear nothing, you who have never feared anything.'

At one point she had stood from her chair at the window and took several steps towards the back wall where the painting was..*waiting*..where the painting was, hanging.

'You do not need to go and see it alone Concetta, soon Alesandro will be home, you do not need to be alone with it at all'

And then the voice came...from somewhere close, too close..

'Can you hear me? Can you hear me? Answer me..'

Edward, or was it Charles? One of the two men in the painting, calling, calling out for her...

Concetta pushed the palms of each hand tightly over her ear's trying to block out the sounds, her eyes tightly closed, the beat of her heart accentuated now feeling like the heavy thuds echoing in her head.

'Mother come to the door, come to the door!'

The commotion now confusing, the thudding in her head slowly moving away into the distance, now coming from a different place, a different direction, the voice now familiar, Alesandro, Alesandro. Concetta swiftly rose from her chair and stumbled towards the sound of what she now knew was someone knocking on the shop's door, having made her way to it she hastily unlocked it, Alexander caught his mother as she virtually fell into his arms. He had been right to come home, he had been right, she had needed him.

--- --- --- --- ---

Under the stark and yet comforting lighting of the overhead fluorescent tube the painting hung with a silent inertia that was total, nothing moved, nothing seemingly movable. They stood side by side, mother and son, deep in their own thoughts. *Nothing moved, nothing movable.* It was with mutual relief when they finally stepped away, Alesandro's hand pausing over the trigger of the light switch before leaving it in the on position.

'What is happening to us Alesandro, why the fear, why the fear now after all these years?'

Across the small room above the shop with the painting hanging amongst it's shelving Alesandro realised that now he knew the answer and it was one he had hoped he would never have to encounter and one he would soon have to reveal to his mother...S.D.E...Spontaneous Dark Essence.

--- --- --- --- ---

It had been the basis of all his endeavours for as long as he could remember, his mother had nurtured it's growth in him, not only a belief in the existence of 'dark essence' but his own unique ability to discover it, realize it and hopefully, eventually, combat it. From a very early age Alexander could see, sense and feel in various objects the potential of this invisible power. Had he not spoken to others on many occasions about his beliefs? Was it not his duty to protect others?

'Is it so far from the realms of comprehension that if an item/object can be of a friendly disposition it could also be of an unfriendly one, if an object can somehow radiate an aura of warmth and well-being it could also be capable of the converse.'

Audiences would listen to him speak on the subject, read about it in his many written articles....

'I believe that it is incredibly rare for an object to radiate any form of 'dark essence' to an unreceptive person or persons, having said that a person given the gift wanted or unwanted of such receptiveness could easily succumb to the 'dark essence' being emitted.'

And then the reason for his searching out the, 'dark essence'... Alexander was frightened, something has been unleashed, something evil has come to the fore and his words came back to haunt him.'

'In my vast experience of dealing with persons affected by this sometimes extreme or violent phenomena, I can assure you that what we talk about being a mere energy can manifest itself into something far more tangible, far more physical - S.D.E. 'Spontaneous Dark Energy'...

--- --- --- --- ---

He had waited until he was sure his mother had retired to her bed, standing quietly outside her bedroom he put his ear to the door the sound of her shallow breathing told him she had finally succumbed to a somewhat fretful sleep. He would take his chance and hope in not waking her. It had been a good few years since he'd been in the small room, his mothers other room and it was just as he had remembered it, the dull light from a single candle and dusty smell of age. The table his mother called her '*altar*' was standing as it always had just a little way from the rooms only window. Alexander went down on all fours and felt for the Ottoman that he knew to be under it. He dragged it out along the floor with a cloud of dry dust and dead insects, careful not to make too much noise. Clear of the '*altar*' he ran his fingers over the Ottomans lid feeling the

ancient etched markings as he carefully lifted it. A strong wave of strangely warm air met his nostrils as he did so. Inside was a length of Hessian laying neatly folded over the familiar leather bag that he and Diogo used for their *work,* a pair of tarnished silver candelabra, a silver pocket watch with shattered dial, a large quilt pen whose feathers ran up his forearm with an almost painful tickle and various other items which no doubt had their own stories to tell. But none of these items were the object of his endeavour, he lifted them out one by one and lay them onto the floor. For one heart stopping moment it seemed to his probing eyes that the Ottoman had relinquished all its secrets and was finally empty. But then he saw it, the tome and even in the duller light of the Ottomans interior he could read its title embossed in gold bold script on a black tattered and frayed cover.

Devotees of Dark Essence Energies

Leaning carefully over the the Ottomans open top Alexander lowered his arms into it, slid his fingers gingerly under the tome and gently lifted it out, he blew a fine layer of dust from it and lay it on the floor away from all the other items. For a long while he knelt on numbing knees just staring at the tome he hadn't set eyes on since he was a small child. The shadow of a memory slowly drifted into his mind, the memory of an inscription written in black fading *italics* on the inside page of the tome, with tentative fingers he turned to it...

Quando il diavolo ti accarezza vuole l' anima...

'When the devil caresses you he wants your soul...'

He would take the tome to the sanctity of his room and study it's pages, scrutinise every word and pray to whichever God it suggested.

--- --- --- --- ---

He was having trouble reading the words of his book, a fugue had taken control of his body and he was reluctant to move. It had been on his mind to switch on the only light in his room for a while but he just hadn't got around to it. It had been a long and tedious journey back and the journey itself fruitless. The 'dark essence' he and Alexander had sought having eluded them, the poor wretched soul of the man requiring it *'be gone'* unfortunately no longer in need of anything at all. Diogo's mind drifted back to the conversation he'd had with Alexander on the train back, when he finally gave vent to his niggling curiosity. *Am I thinking as I feel you are Alexander, that Mr. Patrick's wife and her mother they burn house, they kill Mr. Patrick and take 'dark essence' from house with them?'*

Alexander had turned towards his companion, he had answered Diogo as if he'd been awaiting his question for some time.

'I believe Mr. Patrick's wife killed her husband and then set the house ablaze, I believe her mother was ignorant of all and I believe the statuette was taken by her daughter Abigail. We need to go to her mother's house and we need to go sooner rather than later ....

--- --- --- --- ---

As she quietly made her way down the stairs her hands firmly gripping the bannisters and her head still throbbing with the headache from hell, Abigail could hear her mother's murmuring voice coming from the open door of the lounge. Barbara Raynes was in deep conversation with someone, her voice a mere whisper but Abigail could still make out some of her words...she peered through the crack in the door....'*...don't* *worry....mine now...you and....I understand...together...today I am taking you away with me, away from...'*

Her mother had the statuette of Aesculapius in her arms on the sofa and was cradling it as if it were a baby,....Abigail could barely believe what she was seeing. The headache that had threatened to overwhelm her manifested itself into a red mist of rage.

'Put that back exactly where you found it, how dare you touch my things.'

Abigail's screaming voice sliced through the still air like a knife as she threw herself into the room, both arms outstretched, fingers curled into bony talons. She snatched at the statuette now almost hidden from view in the folded arms at her mothers breast. With no real aim in mind other to protect her *'newly acquired prize'* from her daughter's grasping hands, Barbara, with an agility that belied her age and size leapt from the sofa as Abigail's nails tore shreds of skin from her forearms.

It was hers, the man at the fair gave it to her, it was hers and nobody else's.

'You've won a prize little missie, look, you've won a prize' They were cheering all around her people cheering, chanting.....'She's won a prize look, little missie has won a prize'

With determined strides the older woman forced her weak and aged legs to carry her towards the kitchen area of the house, with the tears now welling up in her eyes blurring her vision she cracked her exposed shins against the low lying edge of the solid wood of a coffee table. Barbara's knees buckled and the blinding pain surging through her body sent her crashing to the floor. Abigail was on her in an instance, pulling her head up backwards by her long hair and grabbing at the statuette now buried between her mothers ample bosom and plump awkwardly positioned arms.

'It is mine you bitch it is mine, give me that god damn thing, how many time do I have to fucking tell you it is mine not yours...'

The continuous ringing of bell on the front door and the loud banging on the window went unnoticed by either woman such was their blind rage.

It was in the middle of a row of old but up market terraced houses in the Keynsham district of Bristol, Alexander found a number of suitable parking places a few houses away from the address scribbled on the note Mel had given him and parked. Taking the old leather bag from the back seat he and Diogo got out of the car and started the short walk to Barbara Rayne's house. It was early morning, the roads were quiet and the pavements empty of pedestrians so when the sounds of loud screaming came to them it was carried on the relative silence.

Both men immediately hastened their step, the sounds were emanating from the very house they were seeking. In an instant they were on the front garden path of the property,

Alexander sidestepped to the front window and peered through, what he saw - two women fighting on the floor of the lounge pawing at each other like feral cats -made him act instinctively, he knocked loudly on the pane of glass in an effort to distract them. Diogo went to the front door and jammed his finger on the bell with one hand and slammed on the brass knocker with the other. After a sideways glance, when he saw that the smaller man had somehow managed to gain entry into the house, Alexander stepped out off the neatly arranged flower bed under the window and made straight towards the disappearing figure of Diogo. The door had been locked but under urgent pressure from Diogo's pushing and kicking finally opened inwards into a wide hall way, Alexander followed as Diogo made his way into the interior of the house, the screaming from the struggling women inside the lounge growing far louder. Diogo was a small man in stature but life in the little village on the banks of the Limia in his homeland was

not easy and had made him strong. The wood and glassed panelled door to the lounge had been forced open too far against its own hinges and hit the wall, some of the glass had cracked and the wood splintered. Diogo was through it in an instant and he wasted no time in stepping forward and grabbing the younger of the two ladies under her arms and pulling her free of the woman beneath her. The screams grew in intensity, animal sounds, high pitched and continuous. Diogo dragged his charge away standing between her and her fellow combatant dodging flailing arms and sharp searching nails as he did so. Barbara Raynes seized her chance. The weight that had been pinning her to floor gone and all else oblivious to her, she drew herself up onto all fours and ignoring the blood seeping from cuts to her face and upper arms started spiderlike towards where she had last seen her beloved statuette lying on the carpet. She had almost reached it when hands from somewhere in the sky reached down and before her eyes snatched it away. The total shock on seeing her prize being so cruelly snatched from her caused her arms to buckle and her legs to spasm and cramp. Barbara's nose broke with a dull crunch as her face thudded into the carpet and the concrete that was underneath it.

Alexander placed the heavy statuette into the leather bag and pulled the drawstring tight as he stepped back towards the lounge door, Abigail still in Diogo's firm grasp screamed obscenities and kicked wildly at the Portuguese man's shins, Barbara remained lying faced down on the carpet muttering incomprehensible words to herself. The two men exchanged glances and unspoken words and then Alexander and the marble statuette of Aesculapius were gone from the house. He didn't have to wait long, the passenger door opened and Diogo breathing heavily and rubbing at bruises on his lower legs took his seat at Alexander's side, he glanced at the back seat and the leather bag lay there bulging with its contents.

It wasn't often that Diogo spoke without at first being spoken to but on this occasion the small man could not hold his tongue, his emotions.

'It is different is it not?'

Alexander knew instinctively what his friend was referring to and again he felt the sensation that had until recently been completely alien to him, it being a cold shiver that ran down his neck and spine.

'It will go into the ground, we will bury at a distance and depth until I have a certain confidence over it, there may be some hoping for ownership of it as we speak, it is a valuable object and apart from anything else we need to...' Alexander searched for appropriate words and could come up with no better than 'smother it'

Diogo, with no answer to give to his friend, spoke to the windscreen as he clicked on his seatbelt...

'So o tempo ira dizer'....Only time will tell.

--- --- --- --- ---

She didn't actually see the ambulance draw up outside the house, all she saw through the kinked fold she'd left in the curtains of her front window was a large yellow shape with distorted red and blue lights flashing. Veronica Davies was still unsure she'd done the right thing even if the policewoman now standing in her lounge had told her numerous times that she had.

'I've never dialled 999 in all my life' she told the officer 'Always kept meself to meself 'specially since my Eric died..don't want no trouble see'

W.P.C. Adams smiled, 'Lets have a nice cup of tea and you can tell me what happened, what you saw and heard'

She'd taken the liberty of requesting a cup of tea, now she was sitting down on the sofa and glad to see the elderly lady smile her approval.

Veronica had placed a tray with tea and a few biscuits on the table in front of them and sat down on the matching easy chair, she felt better, they were just going to have a chat, no-one listening to what she would say. When she saw the police woman get a notebook and pen from her jacket Veronica realised that what she had to say was important...it had been all along.

'Always come across to me a bit of a snob, you know, thinks she's better than anyone else around 'ere..didn't get to know 'er well', just 'morning' and 'nice day' stuff like that'

'Did Mrs. Raynes live alone or did her daughter Abigail live with her?'

Veronica was surprised that the policewoman knew her neighbours name and amazed that she knew Barbara's daughters name as well, she was sure she hadn't told her, but then again *'she was a policewoman I suppose'*.

'Oh no, Abigail lived down south somewhere, not sure where, just down south somewhere, I think she was just visiting'

As she spoke Veronica watched as the policewoman wrote little notes in her book, she waited in silence until the policewoman had finished and was holding her pen up in the air.

'So you knew Mrs. Rayne's daughter, Abigail was visiting, Mrs Davies how did you know Abigail was just visiting?'

Veronica was feeling a little less comfortable now, *I kept meself to meself didn't I ?* She nibbled at a biscuit, placing her open palm under her chin to catch the crumbs.

Just as W.P.C. Adams thought she would have to repeat her question Veronica put her half eaten biscuit back on the plate leaned forward and after a quick glance around to check that the empty room was empty apart from them she whispered...

'Saw Barbara leave in her car, in a hurry she was, then a few hours later she came back with Abigail and some bags and stuff, made a hell of a noise they did, banging the front door and all.'

W.P.C. Adams smiled and took a sip of her cold sugary tea, suggesting with her eyes on Veronica's that she was very interested in hearing her story and that she should carry on but *'please, call me Kate'*.

'Well...Kate.. I always keep meself to meself you know but I couldn't help but hear them talking, loud they were and that Abigail she was shouting, cursing, nasty bit of stuff she is if you ask me'

Again W.P.C. Adams raised her eyebrows but said nothing.

'All night they carried on, must 'ave been at least four o'clock in the morning before I could go to sleep, but I didn't sleep long before they were at it again'

Veronica paused to check the room was still empty with exaggerated sweeps of her head and then carried on...

'Funny noises all night long and me a light sleeper, anyway I was going to bang on the wall and say something but I keep meself to meself, I don't want no trouble or folk thinking I'm a busybody or anything like that...but then the men came and I was glad they did because all I could hear was shouting and screaming from....'

'When did the men come Veronica, did you see them, how many men were there, could you describe them ?'

W.P.C. Adams was quick to interrupt the elderly lady but was immediately aware that maybe she'd asked too many questions

at once, she needn't have worried it actually opened the floodgates...and Veronica was on a roll..

'Now it's not like me to be a busybody or anything like that, I keep meself to meself, but there were two men, one tall and thin the other much shorter, stocky and bald, the tall one was carrying a bag...they were walking very fast, like they were running and I knew they were going to Mrs. Raynes house because I just knew...and I was hoping too because the noise and screaming from the house was just getting louder and louder...' Veronica paused, searched in the large pocket of her housecoat for her inhaler used it and to W.P.C. Adams relief resumed her account 'The two men went in like they owned the place and all I could hear then was more screaming and banging about..I was scared I don't mind telling you...and then the screaming didn't sound so loud and I could hear someone crying...'

The sudden knock on the door made both women jump..Veronica stood up and made her way to her kink in the curtain and peered through, she opened the large window to listen the woman speak.

'Just checking that you are ok, what with the ambulance and all'

Veronica said she was tired but fine thank you, closed the window and turned back into the room..

'It was only Winnie from across the road' she told the still seated policewoman and then she added...

'The nosy bitch.'

When the determined single knock on his door roused him instantly from his reverie he was immediately upright in his chair placing his book on the upturned crate that served as a coffee table. As Diogo made his way cautiously to the locked door there came another knock, whoever the person was standing out on the landing patience was not one of his virtues, the small Portuguese man was ill at ease when he allowed him access. The man was not at all as Diogo had envisaged. He was tall, bearded, slender and dressed in a suit that belonged in the city and not these backstreets full of bandidos and ladroes in his hand he held a large manilla envelope *'Do not bend'* printed in bold red letters across its surface. The man's very persona immediately drawing Diogo's own to the surface, one of subservience.

'My apologies for calling at such an hour without invitation or appointment but I must talk to you regarding a matter of some urgency, I have information that I must impart that could have far reaching consequences and I implore your audience'

Diogo stood opened mouthed, he had never been spoken to in such a manner and he had trouble comprehending the meaning of his uninvited visitor's words such was his accent, all the same he found himself stepping back and gesturing the man enter. Once over the threshold the man was speaking again, a strong German accent now easily discernible.

'Forgive my abruptness but I am addressing Mr. Diogo Macedo

am I not?

Again Diogo could do little more than stare, his mouth opening and closing without a word being spoken, he could not remember the last time anyone had used his surname, he was nodding despite himself...and the man was talking again..

'My name is Tobias Wyles and I would very much like to talk to you' and then already having walked into the room he asked 'May I come in?'

Diogo still in a state of flux directed the man to one of the mismatched armchairs in his room and bade him sit, as he did so he finally found his voice...

'My manners are short, I am not acostumada to people who call at my casa' Would you like a drink of any sort Mr. Wyles?'

The response was immediate and succinct.

'Thank you no and please call me Tobias'

Diogo sat on the opposite armchair as an uncomfortable silence filled the small room, he watched as Tobias Wyles produced a notebook from an inside pocket of his jacket and opened it. He watched as the stranger consulted his wristwatch, cleared his throat and then started speaking. A feeling of heavy trepidation settling in Diogo's stomach.

'I am informed you have the acquaintance of a man who goes by the name Alexander Constantine, a Doctor of sorts I believe, a man responsible for a great deal of articles and publications in the manner of what is referred to as 'Dark Energy' a man I hasten to add not easily traceable and sometimes for reasons better known to himself going by the name of Alesandro.'

The remark was made in a tone Diogo found distinctly unsavoury and somewhat sarcastic, he virtually leapt from his chair, the Portuguese blood in his veins hot, he was no longer prepared to play the subservient, Alexander was his mentor as well as his only real friend, he was loyal only to him.

'You will leave my casa now, I will have nothing to say to you.'

Tobias Wyles instantly raised his hands palms out as if warding off a blow...realising the pique he had engendered in the other man, he spoke on with a great deal more tact..

'Mr. Macedo, Mr. Macedo, please forgive my indelicate approach it is a frightful trait of mine, my sincere apologies, I assure you I am a friend, he reiterated 'I assure you, a friend.'

Diogo hovered over his armchair not certain what his next move should be, Tobias Wyles had remained seated, one of his hands now extended, offered for Diogo to take in his, after an uncomfortable pause on Diogo's part the two men shook hands.

'I wonder if your kind offer of a drink is still open?'

Tobias Wyles was smiling as he spoke, he lay the large envelope at his feet and pushed it to one side, away from any possibility of any one accidentally stepping on it.

The poncha was warming and welcoming and it wasn't long before the reason for Tobias Wyles' calling finally surfaced, he placed his half empty glass on the makeshift table before him and was speaking....

'It is with great urgency that I relate to him information that I have at my disposal, information that Alexander Constantine, sorry Doctor Alexander Constantine, would do well to heed and I have little time to accomplish this aim.'

When Tobias paused for breath he suspected that some of his brashness had returned and in realising it himself he took Diogo's eyes in his and softened his tone.

'Please Mr. Macedo forgive me again, twenty five years in the Bundespolizei and I have acquired an unfortunate manner of articulation...'

Diogo stood, replenished the glasses and sat down again, still somewhat apprehensive about the stranger in his casa and his motives for being there and then the man himself began to explain all.

'I am desperate as I say to relay certain data by any means as possible to Dr. Alesandro Constantine, but before I do I need clarification that this person is definitely the man I hope him to be. It was necessary and deliberate that I initially approach you Mr. Macedo, to ascertain all the facts and verify them'

Tobias Wyles took a sip of his drink, nodded his appreciation of it to Diogo and continued....

'A few months ago I attended a 'talk' by Dr. Constantine and yourself at a place called....' Tobias Wyles paused to consult his notebook now resting in the palm of his hand before resuming..

'Ah, here it is, Bucklebury, a small village in Berkshire'

Ignoring the surprised look that had manifested itself on Diogo's face Mr. Wyles continued...

'The 'talk' was primarily on a subject very close to my heart, that is to say, a subject I have a great interest in, namely 'Dark Essence' and of course the potential dire effects it can be associated with'.

Diogo's surprise was quickly changing again to suspicion and his initial reaction was to put his glass down and go and search out Alexander himself but something in this man's demeanour and his words kept him rooted to the spot. Sounds of echoing voices and footfall's on the stairs outside on the landing had both men pausing to listen, a door slammed shut and the noises became instantly muted. Tobias Wyles took another sip of poncho and continued where he had left off...

'I was particularly interested when Dr. Constantine referred to the rarer phenomenon that is known as S.D.E. or 'Spontaneous Dark Essence' as you yourself had experienced and if I remember correctly gave an excellent account of'.

Diogo was immediately transported back to the long ago sunny day on the river Limia in his homeland of Portugal with his siblings, Acacleto, and Leonor when Acacleto found the tesouro

that would soon to be the cause of so much devastation in his beloved famalia....

Tobias Wyles interrupted Diogo's thoughts with a question that shook the diminutive Portuguese man to the core with its familiarity.

'Have you noticed any change in Dr. Constantine in the recent weeks at all Mr. Macedo? When I say change I mean a shift in his behaviour towards certain items, certain situations?'

Diogo was confused, lost, he opened his mouth to speak but could not find the right words, his mind went back to Alexander's inexplicable behaviour when faced with taking the painting from the wall of the cottage, the way he flinched at touching it...but then his thoughts left him, Tobias Wyles was speaking again.

'Are either you or Dr. Alesandro or Alexander whatever he chooses to call himself acquainted or have ever been acquainted with a Ms. Alison Cleaver and her poor mother or maybe a Mr. Michael Patrick, who had a penchant for auctions and money to spend, maybe you have had dealings with his wife Abigail?'

With a shaking hand and his eyes fixed on Diogo's, he reached for his drink, and inadvertently knocked the glass off the table.

Tobias Wyles totally ignoring the pool of poncha spreading on the carpet amongst the broken shards of glass was relentless in his pursuance...

'You see Diogo, the persons I have mentioned have both had in their possession certain objects that Dr. Alexander and maybe yourself have knowledge of, maybe have even handled...those items being rather unique because of certain extremely unfortunate circumstances.' He paused and then continued his eyes never leaving Diogo's....

'In passing I feel I must inform you that in the pursuit of my investigation I can relate to you that Mrs. Abigail Patrick has been removed from her mother's abode in Bristol and has been committed to a local mental health hospital, her mother Barbara Raynes is faring no better in hospital and I feel it only right that Dr. Alexander be informed of all of this at your earliest convenience'...again another pause before raising his voice slightly...'I would of course have been happy to relay this information to Dr. Alesandro or again Dr. Alexander personally but for reasons I cannot divulge I must rely on you to do this on my behalf.'

Without further explanation Tobias Wyles placed what remained of his poncha carefully on the upturned crate and reached to one side of his chair to retrieve the manilla envelope he had placed there earlier. He had declined Diogo's offer of more poncha and waited patiently as the small Portuguese man took a dust pan and brush to the shards of glass on the carpet and dabbed at the spilt liquid with a dirty cloth. When Diogo had completed his tasks and returned with a replenished glass of his own, Tobias Wyles gently opened the envelope and took out a single large photograph and without looking at it himself

or saying a word slid it across to Diogo. The photograph was old and monochrome, a large crease ran from one corner to the other and another across its centre. The edges were uneven and its sepia hue made the subject matter difficult to see clearly, Diogo moved it closer and studied it carefully now seeing a man a portly man, with long white sideburns and heavy white bushy beard and suddenly Tobias Wyles was speaking....

'His name was Henry Grover Wyles he was an eminent Doctor of the Church, a wealthy land owner, a respected member of the community and a stalwart in all manner of religiousness and righteousness, he was also I am ashamed to admit of the same blood as I.'

Diogo took his eyes from the photograph to look quizzically at Tobias Wyles and then looking back at picture flipped it over and noticed the name and a date scrawled on the back..there was also something scrawled in Latin but Diogo was unable to translate it,Tobias Wyles had more to add...

'He was also a sadistic rapist, an accomplished murderer and a frequent defiler of infants, the man was pure evil in the true meaning of the words.'

Diogo made as if to return the photograph...its former owner was quick to refuse it. The bearded man was silent for a moment allowing Diogo time to absorb this information before commencing..

'But this is not the real reason I show you this photograph my dear Diogo, no that was only an introduction into something far more harrowing, far more pertinent, look into the photograph Diogo, not at it, into it...'What do you see?'

Diogo brought the image even closer to his face and for a few seconds studied it letting his eye's roam over every square millimetre until the breath caught in his throat and his heart began to race.

' Oh meu querido Deus' he whispered...'Oh my dear God'.

--- --- --- --- ---

It was the kind of drizzle that soaked your clothes in an instant and chilled you right through to your bones. As he strode alone, rapidly, along the pitch black streets towards the shop that was Alexander and Concetta's home Diogo held the photograph in its envelope under his heavy coat and pressed it tightly to his chest mindful not to crease it further, the words of Tobias Wyles still ringing in his head...'*Protect it with your life my friend it is the only one in existence and its value in this affair immeasurable, my trust in you is with it's safe deliverance*'

The man called Tobias Wyles had left his home shaking his hand and giving a deep bow (surely it was gratitude) as he did so, he had promised Diogo he would not follow, he would not make any further contact, his work was complete, his obligations met in full. It was then and only then that Diogo had seen the relief in the other man's eyes, the intense relief that Tobias Wyles could no longer conceal. He had involved himself far too deeply

in matters that should not after such a passing of time have been any of his concern, he had put upon himself a burden of such magnitude that he would have to act on it or spend the rest of his short life in the shadow of guilt. That done he was sated, he could return to the Fatherland, which had become his new home and await his death with a clear conscience - the prognosis was two months, the cancer was aggressive.

Part Thirteen

Quando il diavolo ti accarezza vuole l' anima...

'When the devil caresses you he wants your soul...'

He was sitting on the small wooden chair in his room in his mothers shop, the tome with the gold embossed title 'Devotees of Dark Essence Energies' dated 1798 lying open on his old wooden desk and a weak light from a candle fighting to ward off the dark..

Alexander read again the inscription on the inside of the tome and for the thousandth time pondered over the words printed there. 'When the devil caresses you he wants your soul' Those exact words had stayed with him since boyhood. With a cottoned gloved hand he turned the fragile page over to the next one. He was confronted by a long list of grouped numerals running down the centre of the page headed by the words..'Tempus in Numerus'....(time in numbers) he knew these were the dates of the transcribed entries in the tome and he also knew they were all 979ad to 1564ad case histories he had previously endeavoured to decipher into English from Latin. These were of little interest to him today, he briefly scanned them until he got to the tomes back pages and finally what he had been looking for...*Descriptionem in tenebris essentia industria scholarium.* The scholars description of dark essence energy, and below that in his own hand writing a section he had taken from it and converted into English over 40 years ago...

Spontaneous Dark Essence, S.D.E. whereby essence energies are merged and in doing so manifest themselves to become far more powerful, far more potent, the effects virtually 'spontaneous'

For a while Alexander just sat in the silence of his room and stared at that line of words he'd copied all those years before, his eyes were particularly drawn to

'far more powerful, far more potent and spontaneous' and he tried to recall what his thoughts were of when he wrote them.

'It's never going to happen, the chain of coincidences, of probabilities, of indeed evil influences that are requisite for it to occur are far too great to comprehend'

Alexander was opening the tome to a page he had marked many years ago...to an all alleged account of S.D.E. he had translated from Latin to English when he was younger more innocent and eager to learn as much as he could of the rare

phenomenon.......*and it was said that the evil that had befallen them was hurtful and destroying and the evil was given to others that had evil of theirselves and that in the doing of this thing the evils did marry and spawn a greater more deadly mischief..*

Alexander turned to another page...

...he was of evil intent and nor a villager would doubt it, when the maiden was denied to him for purpose of matrimony he secreted on the family a second evil in full knowledge of a first

and death among the entire family was swift and decisive with the said maiden's loss of mind...

And what was to be done to null this coming together of 'dark essences' ?

'the evils did marry and spawn a greater more deadly mischief'...' he secreted on the family a second evil'.. what was to be done if already the dark essences were as one? Could the once lone now co-joined evils be cleaved?

Alexander searched through the remaining pages of the tome studying the ancient text and scribbled notes that persons long before the beginning of his own life had inscribed. Two lines in badly faded Latin with some words or letters missing under a heading...'Dark Energy ....' (the last word completely obliterated) took his eyes and although he struggled with its translation he was confident he was fairly accurate.

Nella vita nella morte insiemie per sempre deve essere, colui che e visitato da questo male condividera la sua tomba con esso..

In life and in death, together forever they must be. He who is visited by this evil will share with it his grave.

Alexander was not aware of the door slowly opening behind him, he was only alerted to the fact that a person had entered his room by the sudden violent flickering of the candles flame.

Concetta lay her hands on her sons shoulders and Alexander immediately felt the warmth of them on his skin, she looked over at the tome laying open on the table and her fingers tightened further on his flesh.

'You are deeply troubled son?'

It was a question not a statement.

--- --- --- --- ---

'If you ask me he hasn't been well for a long time and was getting worse, spent all his time pouring over these books and manuals and hardly ever left this office'

Miranda was arranging said books and manuals into neat piles on the desk, trying to ignore the musty smell that prevailed in the tiny room and the title of one of the book on the top of one pile...*Fact or Fiction the truth about Dark Essence and Death.* Mr. Donaldson was standing in the doorway, he hadn't visited

this particular museum for a while there had never been any reason for him to do so until today.

'So let me get this straight, he just rang up just before closing time last night and told you that because of personal reasons, not because he felt ill, he would not be back, ever'

'That's right Mr. Donaldson, he told me he would drop off all the museums keys through the letter box and he hung up'.

Miranda was pulling open the drawers of the desk one by one, all of which were completely empty as were the small shelves standing on top of it. Mr. Donaldson had entered the room and was studying some papers in his hand.

'He didn't say anything to anybody prior to this..this leaving of his?'

Miranda was now switching on the computer, fully expecting it to ask for a password she would not know. 'No he didn't say anything, he hardly said anything to anybody, seemed to be preoccupied all the time, strange man, really strange, he gave me the creeps'

Mr. Donaldson ignored the secretary's remark ..'Been here over fours years I see in his notes.' Mr. Donaldson flicked the piece of paper with his index finger as he spoke, and then with a deep sigh added...'Well I suppose we need to start looking for a new curator'

Miranda smiled widely as she picked up the triangular piece of shiny plastic that had 'Tobias Wyles Curator..embossed

in black letters on it.

--- --- --- --- ---

'You are deeply troubled'

His mothers question hung in the air until she responded to it herself...'As am I'

They were in the small room on the second floor of *'Concetta's Antiques and Curios'* Alexander looked back over his shoulder and gave a tired smile to his mother, he stood closing the tome as he did so, he had seen and read enough. Together and in silence mother and son placed the leather bag with its carved surface and all the other items back into the Ottoman along with the tome and covered it all once again with the Hessian. Alexander knelt down and carefully slid the Ottoman back into its place under his mothers 'altar'.

Together they left the small room for the larger space of the lounge, it was late, the shop closed and the air pregnant with unuttered words between them.

'You seek answers in the tome? Solace? Concetta did not wait for her son's reply she watched him slump wearily into the nearest chair and continued...

'I feel it also Alexander, I feel a change in the way of things, we need to..'

The heavy banging on the shops door was not only unexpected but jarring, making mother and son jump and stare almost comically into each others eyes. 'Who in Gods name could be calling at this hour?'

--- --- --- --- ---

When Diogo saw the flickering light on the upper floor of the shop his pace quickened as did his heart. He had never visited

Alexander's and Concetta's abode uninvited and certainly not at this late hour of the day but what he had in his possession and what he had to say warranted no delay. The drizzle had mercifully ceased but Diogo still held the envelope as close to his chest as possible, it was without hesitation that he knocked loudly on the shops entrance door, without apprehension he awaited an answer.

--- --- --- --- ---

'And, this man 'Tobias Wyles', you had never seen him before and you know nothing of him?'

They were now sitting at the table in the living quarters of the shop, Concetta was in the kitchen area preparing hot drinks but listening avidly to the conversation between the two men... Diogo had removed his sodden coat, relieved that the envelope still gripped in his hands showed no signs of water damage but sightly uneasy about the looks Alexander was giving him.

'I have never seen the man until when he come to my casa, he know of me and he say he know of you, he say he read of you and he hear of your talkings'

Alexander pushed further..

'How did he know where you lived, what did he want?'

Diogo lowered his eyes to the envelope in his hands and his words were a jumble.

'He say he not sure of where you is live, he say he had little time to be know, he say protect this with your life Diogo.'

Alexander struggled to keep the anxiety from his voice, Diogo was by nature a timid being and easily unsettled, on this occasion he looked far too fragile to interrogate too harshly.

Concetta entered the room with two steaming mugs of tea, handed one to Alexander and waited while Diogo put his envelope carefully on the table top before taking his.

'Obrigada' he said to Concetta looking at her fleetingly before averting his eyes to Alesandro and then again to the envelope before him.'

Alexander spoke knowing the answer to his own question before asking it.

'Is it something we should know about Diogo, if so I think you should show us now'

Concetta had taken a seat near her son and opposite Diogo sipping at her own tea and trying to ignore the unnatural aura that was now so heavy between the three.

'Yes he gave me that, the man he say was Tobias Wyles, I will say to you all what he say to me'...Diogo pointed a stumpy gnarled finger at the envelope and then added 'se voce por favor' ...*if you please'*

--- --- --- --- ---

Mother and son studied the photograph laying on the table before them..it was of an elderly distinguished man dressed in the formal clothing of the era standing in what presumably was his study..his arms and hands at his back, his chest puffed out, he had long white sideburns and a white bushy beard, his countenance was stern....Alexander flipped it over and read the scrawl inked on the back... Henry Grover Wyles...1897. And under those words others that obviously Diogo had not read as they were in Latin..

Et draconi qui est in hominus figura...(A monster in human shape).

Alexander raised his eyebrows, turned the photo back over and looked quizzically at Diogo, who repeated exactly what Tobias Wyles had said to him...

'Look into the photograph Alexander, not at it, into it...what do you see?'

Concetta tore her eyes from the photograph and stared at her son when Alexander gave out a muffled cry.

On the wall behind the man called Henry Grover Wyles hung an all too familiar painting of four people their faces turned away

from the artist and not too far from it standing alone on a shelf a statuette, the marble statuette of a God called Aesculapius.

Alexander ran a finger gingerly over the dry glossy surface of the photograph pausing when it was over the painting partially hidden in the shadows and then over the statuette that seemingly had captured over time a ray of subtle light where there should not have been any.

He was speaking aloud to his mother the thoughts that were running through his mind.

'So at one time and and no-one could know for certain how long Mr.Tobias Wyles had been the custodian of both the painting and the statuette..and no doubt completely ignorant of the evil effect they were having on him...S.D.E.'

Concetta looked down on her son her eyes intent her arms crossed at her chest.

'I will summon him now' she said, 'We have much work to do and to accomplish it will require the *melding,* we will need another mind.'

Alexander said nothing in reply he just nodded his affirmation.

And with that Concetta left the room.

--- --- --- --- ---

It was hanging there, where it had once demanded to be, a silent image so serene that it would be impossible for anybody observing it to think of it as anything but beautiful, innocent, captivating.... a painting. Concetta stared into its oh so familiar scene and defied it to change, to become alive again, to draw her in and take her to its place of existence, to where it lived, it did none of these things. It would not, could not, not with

Alesandro standing at her side *another mind.* Concetta challenged it, she goaded it.

Speak to me Edward, turn from staring at the green hill to face me..and Lizzie is Olivia right when she says you wouldn't know a Sparrowhawk from a Swan ?...and laugh all of you laugh...go on I challenge you.

The painting remained silent, inert, but its essence somehow prevailed and try as she could Concetta could not ignore it. When Alesandro moved to unhook it from the wall her heart missed a beat and she broke out in an all consuming cold sweat. Alesandro carried it up the stairs to it's temporary place in the lounge and placed it on a convenient shelf, it was not to be there for any length of time but he was doing as requested. Concetta watched him place it convinced that at any minute howls of laughter would escape from its canvas.

--- --- --- --- ---

The earth of the '*grave*' was still soft even though after digging it Alexander and Diogo had spent a lot of time flattening it down with their spades. Both men were wary to the possibility of being seen in the field by passing cars but the night was moonless and dark with heavy clouds. The tree they had used

as a marker all those nights ago was wide enough at its base to place the small lantern giving adequate light for their purpose. The statuette had been buried in a shallow 'grave' and it was not long before they reached it wrapped up in its plastic bin bag of which Alexander remembered saying 'such an unfit coffin for something of such unworldly potential'.

Alexander and Diogo kicked the loose dirt from their boots, placed the object of their labours on the back seat of the car and drove off into the early morning light.

--- --- --- --- ---

The hour was late but the shops lights were all illuminated, carrying the heavy weight of the statuette under one arm Alexander unlocked the door and Diogo gently pushed it open. The two men entered and on locking the door behind them made their way to the stairs leading to the rooms above. Voices came to them as they ascended, one male one female, Alexander held the statuette tighter as he entered the shops lounge, Diogo trailing close behind him.

Part Fourteen

'Ah, here we are...Henry Grover Wyles stated as an eminent Doctor of the Church, a wealthy land owner and respected member of the community, born 1842 died 1910 ...Laid to rest,

Flaxen Cemetery, Newbury, in the County of Berkshire...Cause of death...Asphyxia. 'I'm sorry there no more details apart from ...no wait, there is a little bit more'.

April 19th 1911...A horde of local villagers and (lunatics) were arrested whilst apparently desecrating the grave of Henry Grover Wyles. A report states that the grave had been greatly disturbed and the actual body of the deceased assaulted. It was rumoured that a number of heinous crimes were allegedly committed by the deceased throughout his lifetime but no details or evidence of such crimes were ever substantiated.

Alesandro took the notepad on the desk next to the laptop on the library's counter and scribbled down the details, pausing for a while over the given C.O.D. For reasons best known to himself he wrote...'strangulation'

Thanking the young lady who was already hidden behind a mountain of books Alesandro took his leave.

--- --- --- --- ---

Alexander walked across the room, three sets of eyes trained on the innocuous looking creased and dirty black plastic bin bag in his arms shedding grains of dirt and dust onto the carpet. They watched as he slowly revealed its contents by firstly

unravelling the split and clinging plastic and then placing a grubby hand inside to grab the statuette by the base. Now, taking its weight in both hands he carefully placed it on the table in the centre of the room and stood back from it, admiring its undeniable beauty. If anybody had been studying the large old oak barometer on the wall they would have noticed its hand drop by a full two degrees. Concetta stood back, her eyes going from the statuette to the painting now standing unattached on the shelf, she eyed them both with a mixture of awe, fascination and dread. In her imagination she could clearly see the tall portly man standing, posing with his back to the painting, to the statuette, it was the year 1897 and the photographer had just set up his array of camera equipment.

'Dr. Wyles Sir, from the distance you have requested I have in this frame a wide view which contains a fair amount of your surrounding furnitures, and decor would you prefer for me to concentrate solely on your....

'Do as I have requested man take your damned shot from there...

Concetta was alarmed that the images and sounds came to her mind with such vivid clarity....

And then the huge flash of white and the loud and explosive puff sound that accompanied it. It was as real to her as the sound of the shuffling feet that now interrupted her thoughts, that coupled with the sound of her son Alesandro's voice.

'We now have both the objects in the same room just as in the photograph   given to us by the somewhat mysterious Mr. Tobias Wyles, who no doubt was a close relative. Concetta was quick to add, the smile on her face the one of a proud mother..' I also have together in the same room, my identical twin sons...Alexander and Alesandro.' The two men exchanged almost nonchalant nod's of the head. Diogo smiled widely, his love of both men was equal, his eyes went to Concetta, who seemed to be adrift in a dream of her own...

'Concetta mia amata..you must go to England, there is nothing for you here.'

'Please do not say that...there is you Alesandro and this is my casa, mia vita..my home.'

'Sofia has beseeched you Concetta, there will be no life for you here when I am dead.'

Concetta stared into the eyes of her marito, her eyes welling up, her hands spread protectively over her greatly swollen belly.

'Sofia, she has money, she has property in England, my sorella she will take care of you take care of our bambina'

Alesandro raised his head from the sweat stained straw pillow, his dark brown sunken eyes searching Concetta's...

'If you won't do it for me do it for the bambina'

--- --- --- --- ---

'So Concetta lodate il nostro signore you have two, bambine...you cannot name them both Alesandro in honour of your dead husband, that is just not a done thing, people would mock'

It was Sofia, she held one bambina swathed in blankets, Concetta held the other..

'I will name one Alexander...it is fitting, his father Alesandro would be so proud, it would be his English bambina, what father could be more blessed ?

Sofia gave a wry smile she had no answer, no argument.

Although fitting, Concetta had always bemoaned the fact that both men had agreed from a very young age that being two when all others expected one was to their advantage and the evils they encountered eased by the sharing of. What lay ahead of them would test that theory to its limits.

Part Fifteen

'Dark Essence.....'

'Nella vita nella morte insiemie per sempre deve essere, colui che e visitato da questo male condividera la sua tomba con esso..

In life and in death, together forever they must be. He who is visited by this evil will share with it his grave....

They were in the small room, Concetta's room and the tome was lying open on top of her 'altar' the candle light just sufficient to read the salient words.

'There look, is it not written as I suggested, have I misinterpreted it ? I cannot make out its small heading....it looks like as someone down through the ages has deliberately obliterated it....we may never know why.'

It was Alexander nodding his head towards the faint script drawing his brother's attention to it both bending low to squint at each letter.

'Is my translation not correct dear brother? Your Latin teacher always gave me top marks for your work?'

Alexander's quip went without reaction from either man, the shadowed room's sombre ambience would not allow it.

The tome safely put back into the Ottoman with the rest of the items that were contained in it. Alexander slid it back under the 'altar' and without any further words, blew out the candle and followed his brother from the room, both men being deep in thought.

--- --- --- --- ---

Alesandro drove, Alexander in the passenger seat in front of Diogo and Concetta next to him staring out of the window still annoyed by the conversation she'd had earlier that evening with her sons.

'It is our work mother, we are three, we can ...

'Non ne sentireemo piu parlare....I will hear no more about it'

Ma mamma non e posto per te....But mother it is no place for you'

' Saro il giudice quell'Alexaner...I will be the judge of that Alexander.'

Both Alexander and his sibling had heard this tone in their mother's voice before, both knew any further argument would be futile.

The journey would not take long, it was 01.45 and the A roads quiet, Alesandro drove carefully keeping strictly to the imposed speed limits mindful of the precious cargo they were carrying and the questions the authorities would ask if they were stopped. It was as the weather men predicted, clouded over with a slight drizzle and a cold wind..no dog walkers or courting couples especially at this hour. Alesandro pulled up in the exact spot in the winding lane where they had parked the previous night, tight into a natural lay-by created by over hanging trees and a wall of moss covered boulders sunken into a high bank. He switched off the cars engine and lights and immediately the blanket of silence and darkness engulfed them all. As planned Diogo was out of the car first and he went straight to the boot, he opened it and took out the red warning triangles, looking in all direction he placed one at the back and one at the front of the car...Alesandro and Alexander were standing at the boot when he returned. Alexander handed him the spade he had used before still covered in caked mud and took his own, Alesandro had his pick axe in one hand and the spare spade in the other....

'It may still take some time mother, why don't you...'

Alexander was leaning into the opened door of the car, speaking to his mother as she was preparing to leave it...

'And be seen in here if and when someone does pass ?' Besides it is something I have to witness.' Concetta was now out off the car buttoning up her heavy coat 'E che Cristo sia con noi'..and may Christ be with us.

--- --- --- --- ---

All four passed through the small wooden gate hanging open by rusted hinges and then up the uneven grassed over path to the rear of the towering church, Concetta continuously crossing herself, Alexander studying the dark mounds of graves for fresh flowers and seeing none. They rounded the thick trunk of the

Yew tree taking care not to trip over its exposed roots and keeping their tools well away from over hanging branches. Soon they would be at the cemetery's extreme edge and close to the dry stone wall that separated it from a farmer's field, Alexander once again with the feeling that it was shear providence that anyone had chosen to bury this man where they did. When they finally reached the grave that had at first taken them such a long time to locate Alesandro let out a huge silent sigh, the surface topsoil they had so carefully spread was untouched, under it the tarpaulin pinned to the sheet of thin plywood undisturbed..the sods of lose earth spread about in the surrounding bushes invisible unless deliberately looked for.. their arduous labours of the last few nights obviously gone undetected.

Concetta having not seen it before stared at the chipped and desecrated headstone with its stark inscription and moss covered surface poking up from the ground at an awkward angle like a decaying tooth in an infected gum.

Henry Grover Wyles

1842-1910

Inadequately illuminated by the single lantern placed by the graves now discernible edge Diogo and Alexander knelt at each side and taking hold of the tarpaulin covered plywood by its edges pulled it aside careful not to pour its covering soil back into the airless cavity below. Diogo was already lowering himself into the depths spade in hand, there was still an amount of earth to be excavated and the diminutive Portuguese man was eager to have it done and be gone from Este lugar de morte.... *this place of death.*

Alesandro followed the smaller man sliding down the damp mud of the earth walls into the black abyss, Alexander held the lantern high spreading and making the most of its weak light, Concetta stood completely still in the cold drizzle in silent prayer and below her feet, despite the cramped conditions the toiling men were nearing the...

…..and that's when the low rumbling sound first reached their ears and stilled their movements instantly, each looked at the other and heartbeats quickened.

'This'll do, can't get any further into fucking nowhere than this.'

The man with the heavily tattooed arm reached for the passenger's door and had it open before vehicle came to a complete stop.

'Keep it quiet, lets just get on with it and turn those fucking lights off '

The man with the long grey hair tied at the back of his head with a red band slid the vans side door open and pulled out the first two tyres he could reach and swearing under his breath, he threw them into the bushes. It took them almost half an hour to completely empty the van and both men despite the drizzle that was persistent were sweating profusely.

'Right, lets get the fuck out of here'

No more than a few yards down the narrow lane they passed a car parked and almost most hidden amongst the trees in a lay by. Neither man saw it.

--- --- --- --- ---

The moon had found a way through the slowly drifting night clouds and a dull silvery light refracting off the cold drizzle put a grey shroud over all before her. On the ground beside the black maw of the open grave a spade lay redundant, abandoned by its owner as he had no doubt fled in sheer terror from what he had just witnessed. Concetta could do nothing, her bones had locked in a state of rigour mortise that was total, her heart a cold lump in her chest....and then the arm about her shoulders and the voice in her ear....

Concetta opened her eyes and just caught herself before a wave of dizziness caused her knees to buckle..in an instant her senses came back to her, for a while it had seemed she had lost conscientiousness, now it was dark, no moon, no silvery light, no spade lying in the grass and Alexander standing at her side a deeply concerned look on his face.

'They have gone mother, those people out on the lane have gone...and we still have work to do, I will take you back to the car, you look so pale, you are both cold and damp from the drizzle, here let me...'

'No non lo farai... no, no, you will not...Concetta's response was instant and urgent, for a brief second Alexander was worried that her voice had carried too far. Concetta must have seen the alarm on her sons face when she spoke again it was in a whisper...

'I am going nowhere Alexander, I am staying here, I have to see this through to the end...'

'Alexander', it was Alesandro and his voice came from somewhere in a dense mist that had appeared suddenly from nowhere 'We are getting nearer fratello, we are almost there. Mother and son took faltering steps toward the black rectangle that was an open grave and Diogo, the smaller of the men still labouring with a spade but now completely hidden from view.

No birdsong, no sound, just imagined silhouettes in the clinging mist of long ago, mourners their shoulders slumped, their eyes down, black top hats of the men and the black net veils of the women lowered to cover alabaster and tear stained faces. The rector at their head standing solemn, an opened book in his hand trailing a red ribbon from its pages, his mouth opening and closing in silent lament. And on the gravel path the carriage it's single horse frozen in time a plume standing erect on its head, its silver bit glinting in the moonlight... Concetta shook the hallucination from her mind she was now as close to the graves hungry mouth as she wanted to be, hers was not to look upon a pile of abandoned bones, hers was to bestow upon the previous owner of those bones what he richly deserved, even after death had taken him. Alesandro paused to lean on his spade and used the sleeve of his heavily soiled cotton shirt to wipe the sweat from his eyes, the freshly hewed mud of the grave walls only inches from his face it's ripe earthy scent assailing his nostrils. When Diogo suddenly lurched sideways and downward in a rapid jerking movement his shoulder inadvertently rammed into Alesandro's exposed flank the taller man knew exactly what had happened. Under their combined weight the rotted wood of the coffin had collapsed crashing down into the brittle bones of the rib cage below causing it to implode like a birds brittle cane aviary. The two men had finally reached the end of their dig. Diogo with Alesandro's arm around his shoulder for balance pulled and shook his booted foot from the hole in the mulch that had once been solid pine murmuring in Portuguese under his breath.

Above on the rough grass standing next to his mother Alexander's brow creased as he looked towards the dark shape of the church. Where once was a black recess in its wall, he could see an arched doorway slated oak and rusted horizontal hinges - the night was rapidly becoming day. And then from some direction almost impossible to ascertain, his siblings hushed voice came to him..

'Alexander we are ready, it is done, hurry, bring them to us, now!'

--- --- --- --- ---

If Alexander had answered his brother neither Alesandro or Diogo had heard him, all they could hear in the dank confines of the grave was their own hearts beating and the terrible squelching and sucking noises merged with the cracking of bone each time they moved their feet. Scaling up the steep and wet mud walls of Henry Grover Wyles final resting place seemed an impossibility...refusing the terrible urge to look down another impossibility....when he eventually did Alesandro's blood ran cold and ice cold shivers ran up and down his already taut spine. The intact skull had been set back in a small carefully constructed cut out in the graves wall a foot or so from the mixture of mud and crushed bones at its base. Through the centre of the skulls forehead was a rusted metal rod. It had no doubt been hammered into the man's head in situ before or even after the grave had been filled, had there not been something about a desecration ?...

Alesandro tore his eyes from the horrific scene knowing full well it would visit him frequently in the nights to follow. Concetta carried the marble statuette, it was heavier but less cumbersome than the painting, she gingerly followed her son, eyes trained on nothing at all but his back, Alexander's frequent glances behind affirmed to him she was keeping pace. As they neared the church the crows high up amongst the gargoyles and grotesques began a chorus of startled cawing as hundreds of feet below them two black shapes had appeared as if from

nowhere out of the dissipating mist. Alesandro made a stirrup of his hands and hoisted a much relieved Diogo from the thing that had become no more than a hole in the ground, no sooner had he done that than his brother's arm appeared silhouetted against a lightening sky. After a few sliding steps against the wet walls of hell it was with grateful thanks that Alesandro found himself in the fresh air alongside his mother and brother.

Nella vita nella morte insiemie per sempre deve essere, colui che e visitato da questo male condividera la sua tomba con esso..

.....In life and in death, together forever they must be. He who is visited by this evil will share with it his grave....

There was little finesse when it came to disposing of the objects of 'Dark Essence'....time was not on their side and there was much to do.

Concetta had insisted on walking to the edge of the grave and unceremoniously dropping the painting into it, she stood and listened as hit the loose earth below, a more than suitable place for it to rot away. Alexander held the statuette of Aesculapius aloft for a few seconds as he eyed Alesando and Diogo in turn before it too was thrown down into the depths.

Spades were quickly utilised and the thud of wet earth landing on wet earth slowly extinguished the other sound....the one Concetta could not avoid listening to...

'Oh now come on my dear chap, just ask our Lizzie...

'Now don't bring me into this Charles, you know I know nothing of birds'

'Olivia, dearest, tell them to cease'

'Edward, for pity's sake'..........thud …..thud ….thud, thud.

Kim Clover...26th July 2021.

Printed in Great Britain
by Amazon